ASSIGNMENT IN ETERNITY

*Also by Robert Heinlein and available
in the NEL series:*

PODKAYNE OF MARS
THE MOON IS A HARSH MISTRESS
THE MAN WHO SOLD THE MOON
THE WORLDS OF ROBERT HEINLEIN
BETWEEN PLANETS
SPACE FAMILY STONE
STRANGER IN A STRANGE LAND
STARSHIP TROOPERS
SPACE CADET
STAR BEAST
ROCKETSHIP GALILEO
HAVE SPACE SUIT — WILL TRAVEL
GLORY ROAD
METHUSELAH'S CHILDREN
REVOLT IN 2100
THE DAY AFTER TOMORROW
I WILL FEAR NO EVIL

Assignment in Eternity

Robert Heinlein

NEW ENGLISH LIBRARY
TIMES MIRROR

For
SPRAGUE and CATHERINE

First published in Great Britain by The Museum Press, Ltd.
© Robert Heinlein

*

FIRST NEL PAPERBACK EDITION MAY 1971
Reprinted December 1973

NEL Books are published by
New English Library Limited from Barnard's Inn, Holborn, London, E.C.1.
Made and printed in Great Britain by Hunt Barnard Printing Ltd., Aylesbury, Bucks.

45000677 8

Gulf

THE first-quarter rocket from Moonbase put him down at Pied-a-Terre. The name he was travelling under began – by foresight – with the letter 'A'; he was through port inspection and into the shuttle tube to the city ahead of the throng. Once in the tube car he went to the men's washroom and locked himself in.

Quickly he buckled on the safety belt he found there, snapped its hooks to the wall fixtures, and leaned over awkwardly to remove a razor from his bag. The surge caught him in that position; despite the safety belt he bumped his head – and swore. He straightened up and plugged in the razor. His moustache vanished; he shortened his sideburns, trimmed the corners of his eye-brows and brushed them up.

He towelled his hair vigorously to remove the oil that had sleeked it down, combed it loosely into a wavy mane. The car was now riding in a smooth, unaccelerated 300 m.p.h.; he let himself out of the safety belt without unhooking it from the walls and, working very rapidly, peeled off his moonsuit, took from his bag and put on a tweedy casual outfit suited to outdoors on Earth and quite unsuited to Moon Colony's air-conditioned corridors.

His slippers he replaced with walking shoes from the bag; he stood up. Joel Abner, commercial traveller, had disappeared; in his place was Captain Joseph Gilead, explorer, lecturer, and writer. Of both names he was the sole user; neither was his birth name.

He slashed the moonsuit to ribbons and flushed it down the water closet, added 'Joel Abner's' identification card; then peeled a plastic skin off his travel bag and let the bits follow the rest. The bag was now pearl grey and rough, instead of dark brown and smooth. The slippers bothered him; he was afraid they might stop up the car's plumbing. He contented himself with burying them in the waste receptacle.

The acceleration warning sounded as he was doing this; he barely had time to get back into the belt. But, as the car plunged into the solenoid field and surged to a stop, nothing remained of Joel Abner but some unmarked underclothing, very ordinary toilet articles, and nearly two dozen spools of micro-film equally appropriate — until examined — to a commercial traveller or a lecture-writer. He planned not to let them be examined as long as he was alive.

He waited in the washroom until he was sure of being last man out of the car, then went forward into the next car, left by its exit, and headed for the lift to the ground level.

'New Age Hotel, sir,' a voice pleaded near his ear. He felt a hand fumbling at the grip of his travel bag.

He repressed a reflex to defend the bag and looked the speaker over. At first glance he seemed an under-sized adolescent in a smart uniform and a pillbox cap. Further inspection showed premature wrinkles and the features of a man at least forty. The eyes were glazed. A pituitary case, he thought to himself, and on the hop as well. 'New Age Hotel,' the runner repeated. 'Best mechanos in town, chief. There's a discount if you're just down from the moon.'

Captain Gilead, when in town as Captain Gilead, al-ways stayed at the old Savoy. But the notion of going to the New Age appealed to him; in that incredibly huge, busy, and ultra-modern hostelry he might remain un-noticed until he had had time to do what had to be done.

He disliked mightily the idea of letting go his bag. Nevertheless it would be out of character not to let the runner carry the bag; it would call attention to himself — and the bag. He decided that this unhealthy runt could

6

not outrun him even if he himself were on crutches; it would suffice to keep an eye on the bag.

'Lead on comrade,' he answered heartily, surrendering the bag. There had been no hesitation at all; he had let go the bag even as the hotel runner reached for it.

'Okay, chief.' The runner was first man into an empty lift; he went to the back of the car and set the bag down beside him. Gilead placed himself so that his foot rested firmly against his bag and faced forward as other travellers crowded in. The car started.

The lift was jammed; Gilead was subjected to body pressures on every side – but he noticed an additional, unusual, and uncalled-for pressure behind him.

His right hand moved suddenly and clamped down on a skinny wrist and a hand clutching something. Gilead made no further movement, nor did the owner of the hand attempt to draw away or make any objection. They remained so until the car reached the surface. When the passengers had spilled out he reached behind him with his left hand, recovered his bag and dragged the wrist and its owner out of the car.

I was, of course, the runner; the object in his fist was Gilead's wallet. 'You durn near lost that, chief,' the runner announced with no show of embarrassment. 'It was falling out of your pocket.'

Gilead liberated the wallet and stuffed it into an inner pocket. 'Fell right through the zipper,' he answered cheerfully, 'Well, let's find a cop.'

The runt tried to pull away. 'You got nothing on me!'

Gilead considered the defence. In truth, he had nothing. His wallet was already out of sight. As to witnesses, the other lift passengers were already gone – nor had they seen anything. The lift itself was automatic. He was simply a man in the odd position of detaining another citizen by the wrist. And Gilead himself did not want to talk to the police.

He let go that wrist. 'On your way, comrade. We'll call it quits.'

7

The runner did not move. 'How about my tip?'

Gilead was beginning to like this rascal. Locating a loose half credit in his change pocket he flipped it at the runner, who grabbed it out of the air but still didn't leave. 'I'll take your bag now. Gimme.'

'No, thanks, chum. I can find your delightful inn without further help. One side, please.'

'Oh, yeah? How about my commission? I gotta carry your bag, else how they gonna know I brung you in? Gimme.'

Gilead was delighted with the creature's unabashed insistence. He found a two-credit piece and passed it over. 'There's your cumshaw. Now beat it, before I kick your tail up around your shoulders.'

'You and who else?'

Gilead chuckled and moved away down the concourse toward the station entrance to the New Age Hotel. His subconscious sentries informed him immediately that the runner had not gone back toward the lift as expected, but was keeping abreast him in the crowd. He considered this. The runner might very well be what he appeared to be, common city riff-raff who combined casual thievery with his overt occupation. On the other hand –

He decided to unload. He stepped suddenly off the sidewalk into the entrance of a drugstore and stopped just inside the door to buy a newspaper. While his copy was being printed, he scooped up, apparently as an after-thought, three standard pneumo mailing tubes. As he paid for them he palmed a pad of gummed address labels.

A glance at the mirrored wall showed him that his shadow had hesitated outside but was still watching him. Gilead went on back to the shop's soda fountain and slipped into an unoccupied booth. Although the floor show was going on – a remarkably shapely ecdysiast was working down toward her last string of beads – he drew the booth's curtain.

Shortly the call light over the booth flashed discreetly; he called, 'Come in!' A pretty and very young waitress

8

came inside the curtain. Her plastic costume covered without concealing.

She glanced around. 'Lonely?'

'No thanks, I'm tired.'

'How about a redhead, then? Real cute –'

'I really am tired. Bring me two bottle of beer un-opened, and some pretzels.'

'Suit yourself, sport.' She left.

With speed he opened the travel bag, selected nine spools of microfilm, and loaded them into the three mailing tubes, the tubes being of the common three-spool size. Gilead then took the filched pad of address labels, addressed the top one to 'Raymond Calhoun, P.O. Box 1060, Chicago,' and commenced to draw with great care in the rectangle reserved for electric-eye sorter. The address he shaped in arbitrary symbols intended not to be read, but to be scanned automatically. The hand-written address was merely a precaution, in case a robot sorter should reject his hand-drawn symbols as being imperfect and thereby turn the tube over to a human postal clerk for readdressing.

He worked fast, but with the care of an engraver. The waitress returned before he had finished. The call light warned him; he covered the label with his elbow and kept it covered.

She glanced at the mailing tubes as she put down the beer and a bowl of pretzels. 'Want me to mail those?'

He had another instant of split-second indecision. When he had stepped out of the tube car he had been reasonably sure, first that the *persona* of Joel Abner, commercial traveller, had not been penetrated, and, second, that the transition from Abner to Gilead had been accomplished without arousing suspicion. The pocket-picking episode had not alarmed him, but had caused him to reclassify those two propositions from calculated certainties to unproved variables. He had proceded to test them once; they were now calculated certainties again – of the opposite sort. Ever since he had spotted his erstwhile porter, the New Age runner, as standing outside this same drugstore his subconscious had been clanging like a burglar alarm.

It was clear not only that he had been spotted but that they were organised with a completeness and shrewdness he had not believed possible.

But it was mathematically probable to the point of certainty that they were not operating through this girl. They had no way of knowing that he would choose to turn aside into this particular drugstore. That she could be used by them he was sure – and she had been out of sight since his first contact with her. But she was clearly not bright enough, despite her alley-cat sophistication, to be approached, subverted, instructed and indoctrinated to the point where she could seize an unexpected opportunity, all in a space of time merely adequate to fetch two bottles of beer. No, this girl was simply after a tip. Therefore she was safe.

But her costume offered no possibility of concealing three mailing tubes, nor would she be safe crossing the concourse to the post office. He had no wish that she be found tomorrow morning dead in a ditch.

'No,' he answered immediately. 'I have to pass the post office anyway. But it was a kind thought. Here.' He gave her a half credit.

'Thanks.' She waited and stared meaningfully at the beer. He fumbled again in his change pocket, found only a few bits, reached for his wallet and took out a five-pluton note.

'Take it out of this.'

She handed him back three singles and some change.

He pushed the change towards her, then waited, frozen, while she picked it up and left. Only then did he hold the wallet closer to his eyes.

It was not his wallet.

He should have noticed it before, he told himself. Even though there had been only a second from the time he had taken it from the runner's clutched fingers until he had concealed it in a front pocket, he should have known it – known it and forced the runner to disgorge, even if he had had to skin him alive.

But why was he sure that it was not his wallet? It was the proper size and shape, the proper weight and feel – real ostrich skin in these days of synthetics. There was the weathered ink stain which had resulted from carrying a leaky stylus in the same pocket. The was a V-shaped scratch on the front which had happened so long ago he did not recall the circumstances.

Yet it was not his wallet.

He opened it again. There was the proper amount of money, there were what seemed to be his Explorers' Club card and his other identity cards, there was dog-eared flat-photo of a mare he had once owned. Yet the more the evidence showed it was his, the more certain he became that it was not his. These things were forgeries, they did not *feel* right.

There was one way to find out. He flipped a switch provided by a thoughtful management; the booth became dark. He took out his penknife and carefully slit a seam back of the billfold pocket. He dipped a finger into a secret pocket thus disclosed and felt around; the space was empty – nor in this case had the duplication of his own wallet been quite perfect; the space should have been lined, but his fingers encountered rough leather.

He switched the light back on, put the wallet away, and resumed his interrupted drawing. The loss of the card which should have been in the concealed pocket was annoying, certainly awkward, and conceivably disastrous, but he did not judge that the information on it was jeopardised by the loss of the wallet. The card was quite featureless unless examined by black light; if exposed to visible light – by someone taking the real wallet apart, for example – it had the disconcerting quality of bursting explosively into flame.

He continued to work, his mind busy with the wider problems of why they had taken so much trouble to try to keep him from knowing that his wallet was being stolen – and the still wider and more disconcerting question of why they had bothered with *his* wallet. Finished, he stuffed the remainder of the pad of address labels into a crack between cushions in the booth, palmed the label he had prepared, picked up the bag and the three mailing tubes. One tube he kept separate from the others by a finger.

No attack would take place, he judged, in the drug store. The crowded concourse between himself and the post office he would have ordinarily have considered equally safe – but not today. A large crowd of people, he knew, are equal to so many trees as witnesses if the dice were loaded with any sort of a diversion.

He slanted across the bordering sidewalk, and headed directly across the middle towards the post office, keeping as far from other people as he could manage. He had become aware of two men converging on him when the expected diversion took place.

It was a blinding light and a loud explosion, followed by screams and startled shouts. The source of the explosion he could imagine; the screams and shouts were doubtless furnished free by the public. Being braced, not for this, but for anything, he refrained even from turning his head.

The two men closed rapidly, as on cue.

Most creatures and almost all humans fight only when pushed. This can lose them decisive advantage. The two men made no aggressive move of any sort, other than to come close to Gilead – nor did they ever attack. Gilead kicked the first of them in the knee-cap, using the side of his foot, a much more certain stroke than with the toe. He swung with his travel bag against the other at the same time, not hurting him but bothering him, spoiling his timing. Gilead followed it with a heavy kick to the man's stomach.

The man whose knee-cap he had ruined was on the

pavement, but still active – reaching for something, a gun or a knife. Gilead kicked him in the head and stepped over him, continued towards the post office.

Slow march – slow march all the way! He must not give the appearance of running away; he must be the perfect respectable citizen, going about his lawful occasions.

The post office came close, and still no tap on the shoulder, no denouncing shout, no hurrying footsteps. He reached the post office, was inside. The opposition's diversion had worked, perfectly – but for Gilead, not for them.

There was a short queue at the addressing machine. Gilead joined it, took out his stylus and wrote addresses on the tubes while standing. A man joined the queue almost at once; Gilead made no effort to keep him from seeing what address he was writing: it was 'Captain Joseph Gilead, the Explorers' Club, New York.' When it came his turn to use the symbol printing machine he made no effort to conceal what keys he was punching – and the symbol address matched the address he had written.

He worked somewhat awkwardly as the previously prepared gummed label was still concealed in his left palm.

He went from the addressing machine to the mailing receivers; the man who had been behind him in line followed him without pretending to address anything.

Thwonk! and the first tube was away with a muted implosion of compressed air. *Thwonk!* again and the second was gone – and at the same time Gilead grasped the last one in his left hand, sticking the gummed label down firmly over the address he had just printed on it. Without looking at it he made sure by touch that it was in place, all corners seated, then *thwonk!* it joined its mates.

Gilead turned suddenly and trod heavily on the feet

of the man crowded close behind him. 'Wups! pardon me,'
he said happily and turned away. He was feeling very
cheerful; not only had he turned his dangerous charge
over into the care of a mindless, utterly reliable automatic
machine which could not be coerced, bribed, drugged,
nor subverted by any other means and in whose com-
plexities the tube would be perfectly hidden until it
reached a destination known only to Gilead, but also he
had just stepped on the corns of one of the opposition.

On the steps of the post office he paused beside a
policeman who was picking his teeth and staring out at
a cluster of people and an ambulance in the middle of
the concourse. 'What's up?' Gilead demanded.

The cop shifted his toothpick. 'First some damm fool
sets off fireworks,' he answered, 'then two guys get in a
fight and blame near ruin each other.'

'My goodness!' Gilead commented and set off diagon-
ally towards the New Age Hotel.

He looked around for his pickpocket friend in the
lobby, did not see him. Gilead strongly doubted if the runt
were on the hotel's staff. He signed in as Captain Gilead,
ordered a suite appropriate to the *persona* he was wearing, and let himself be conducted to the lift.

Gilead encountered the runner coming down just as
he and his bellman were about to go up. 'Hi, Shorty!'
he called out while deciding not to eat anything in this
hotel. 'How's business?'

The runt looked startled, then passed him without
answering, his eyes blank. It was not likely, Gilead considered, that the runt would be used after being detected;
therefore some sort of drop box, call station, or head-
quarters of the opposition was actually inside the hotel.
Very well, that would save everybody a lot of useless com-
muting – and there would be fun for all!

In the meantime he wanted a bath.

In his suite he tipped the bellman who continued to
linger.

14

'Want some company?'

'No, thanks, I'm a hermit.'

'Try this then.' The bellman inserted Gilead's room key in the stereo panel, fiddled with the controls, the entire wall lighted up and faded away. A svelte blonde creature, backed by a chorus line, seemed about to leap into Gilead's lap. 'That's not a tape,' the bellman went on, that's a live transmission direct from the Tivoli. We got the best equipment in town.'

'So you have,' Gilead agreed, and pulled out his key. The picture blanked; the music stopped. 'But I want a bath, so get out – now that you've spent four credits of my money.'

The bellman shrugged and left. Gilead threw off his clothes and stepped into the 'fresher.' Twenty minutes later, shaved from ear to toe, scrubbed, soaked, sprayed, pummelled, rubbed, scented, powdered, and feeling ten years younger, he stepped out. His clothes were gone.

His bag was still there; he looked it over. It seemed okay, itself and contents. There were the proper number of microfilm spools – not that it mattered. Only three of the spools mattered and they were already in the mail. The rest were just shrubbery, copies of his own public lectures. Nevertheless, he examined one of them, unspooling a few frames.

It was one of his own lectures all right – but not one he had had with him. It was one of his published transcriptions available in any large book store. 'Pixies everywhere,' he remarked and put it back. Such attention to detail was admirable.

'Room service!'

The service panel lighted up. 'Yes, sir?'

'My clothes are missing. Chase 'em up for me.'

'The valet has them, sir.'

'I didn't order valet service. Get 'em back.'

The girl's voice and face were replaced, after a slight delay, by those of a man. 'It is not necessary to order valet service here, sir. "A New Age guest receives the best." '

'Okay, get 'em back – chop, chop! I've got a date with the Queen of Sheba.'

'Very good, sir.' The image faded.

With wry humour, he reviewed his situation. He had already made the possible fatal error of underestimating his opponent through – he now knew – visualising that opponent in the unimpressive person of 'the runt.' Thus he had allowed himself to be diverted; he should have gone anywhere rather than to the New Age, even to the old Savoy, although that hotel, being a known stamping ground of Captain Gilead, was probably as thoroughly booby-trapped by now as this palatial dive.

He must not assume that he had more than a few more minutes to live. Therefore he must use those few minutes to tell his boss the destination of the three important spools of microfilm. Thereafter, if he still were alive, he must replenish his cash to give him facilities for action – the amount of money in 'his' wallet, even if it were returned, was useless for any major action. Thirdly, he must report in, close the present assignment, and be assigned to his present antagonists as a case in themselves, quite aside from the matter of the microfilm.

Not that he intended to drop Runt & Company even if not assigned to them. True artists were scarce – nailing him down by such a simple device as stealing his pants! He loved them for it and wanted to see more of them, as violently as possible.

Even as the image on the room service panel faded he was punching the scrambler keys on the room's communicator desk. It was possible – certain – that the scramble code he used would be repeated elsewhere in the hotel and the supposed privacy attained by scrambling thereby breached at once. This did not matter, he would have his boss disconnect and call back with a different scramble from the other end. To be sure, the call code of

16

the station to which he was reporting would thereby be breached, but it was more than worthwhile to expend and discard one relay station to get his message through.

Scramble pattern set up, he coded – not New Washington, but the relay station he had selected. A girl's face showed on the screen. 'New Age service, sir. Were you scrambling?'

'Yes.'

'I am veree sorree, sir. The scrambling circuits are being repaired. I can scramble for you from the main board.'

'No thanks, I'll call in clear.'

'I yam ve-ree sor-ree, sir.'

There was one clear-code he could use – to be used only for crash priority. This was crash priority. Very vell –

He punched the keys again without scrambling and waited. The same girl's face appeared presently. 'I am verree sorree, sir; that code does not reply. May I help you?'

'You might send up a carrier pigeon.' He cleared the board.

The cold breath on the back of his neck was stronger now; he decided to do what he could to make it awkward to kill him just yet. He reached back into his mind and coded in clear the *Star-Times*.

No answer.

He tried the *Clarion* – again no answer.

No point in beating his head against it; they did not intend to let him talk outside to anyone. He rang for a bellman, sat down in an easy chair, switched it to 'shallow massage,' and luxuriated happily in the chair's tender embrace. No doubt about it; the New Age did have the best mechanos in town – his bath had been wonderful; this chair was superb. Both the recent austerities of Moon Colony and the probability that this would be his last massage added to his pleasure.

The door dilated and a bellman came in – about his

own size, Gilead noted. The man's eyebrows went up a fraction of an inch on seeing Glead's oyster-naked condition. 'You want company?'

Gilead stood up and moved towards him. 'No, dearie,' he said grinning, 'I want you' – at which he sank three stiffened fingers in the man's solar plexus.

As the man grunted and went down Gilead chopped him in the side of the neck with the edge of his hand.

The shoulders of the jacket were too narrow and the shoes too large; nevertheless two minutes later 'Captain Gilead' had followed 'Joel Abner' to oblivion and Joe temporary and freelance bellman, let himself out of the room. He regretted not being able to leave a tip with his predecessor.

He sauntered past the passenger lifts, firmly misdirected a guest who had stopped him, and found the service elevator. By it was a door to the 'quick drop.' He opened it, reached out and grasped a waiting pulley belt, and, without stopping to belt himself into it, contenting himself with hanging on, he stepped off the edge. In less time than it would have taken him to parachute the drop he was picking himself up off the cushions in the hotel basement and reflecting that lunar gravitation surely played hob with a man's leg muscles.

He left the drop room and started out in an arbitrary direction, but walking as if he were on business and belonged where he was – any exit would do and he would find one eventually. He wandered in and out of the enormous pantry, then found the freight door through which the pantry was supplied.

When he was thirty feet from it, it closed and an alarm sounded. He turned back.

He encountered two policemen in one of the many corridors under the giant hotel and attempted to brush on past them. One of them stared at him, then caught his arm. 'Captain Gilead –'

Gilead tried to squirm away, but without showing any skill in the attempt. 'What's the idea?'

'You are Captain Gilead.'

'And you're my Aunt Sadie. Let go of my arm, copper.'

The policeman fumbled in his pocket with his other hand, pulled out a notebook. Gilead noted that the other officer had moved a safe ten feet away and had a Markheim gun trained on him.

'You, Captain Gilead,' the first officer droned, 'are charged on a sworn complaint with uttering a counterfeit five-pluton note at or about thirteen hours this date at the Grand Concourse drug store in this city. You are cautioned to come peacefully and are advised that you need not speak at this time. Come along.'

The charge might or might not have something to it, thought Gilead; he had not examined closely the money in the substitued wallet. He did not mind being booked, now that the microfilm was out of his possession; to be in an ordinary police station with nothing more sinister to cope with than crooked cops and dumb desk sergeants would be easy street compared with Runt & Company searching for him.

On the other hand, the situation was too pat, unless the police had arrived close on his heels and found the stripped bellman, gotten his story and started searching.

The second policeman kept his distance and did not lower the Markheim gun. That made other consideration academic. 'Okay, I'll go,' he protested. 'You don't have to twist my arm that way.'

They went up to the weather level and out to the street – and not once did the second cop drop his guard. Gilead relaxed and waited. A police car was balanced at the curb. Gilead stopped. 'I'll walk,' he said. 'The nearest station is just around the corner. I want to be booked in my own precinct.'

He felt a teeth-chattering chill as the blast from the Markheim hit him; he pitched forward on his face.

He was coming to, but still could not co-ordinate, as they lifted him out of the car. By the time he found himself being half-carried, half-marched down a long corridor he was almost himself again, but with a gap in his memory. He was shoved through a door which clanged behind him. He steadied himself and looked around.

'Greetings, friend,' a resonant voice called out. 'Drag up a chair by the fire.'

Gilead blinked, deliberately slowed himself down, and breathed deeply. His healthy body was fighting off the effects of the Markheim bolt; he was almost himself.

The room was a cell, old-fashioned, almost primitive. The front of the cell and the door were steel bars; the walls were concrete. Its only furniture, a long wooden bench, was occupied by the man who had spoken. He was fiftyish, of ponderous frame, heavy features set in a shrewd, good-natured expression. He was lying back on the bench, he pillowed on his hands, in animal ease. Gilead had seen him before.

'Hello, Dr. Baldwin.'

The man sat up with a flowing economy of motion that moved his bulk as little as possible. 'I'm not Dr. Baldwin – I'm not Doctor anything, though my name is Baldwin.' He stared at Gilead. 'But I know you – seen some of your lectures.'

Gilead cocked an eyebrow. 'A man would seem naked around the Association of Theoretical Physicists without a doctor's degree – and you were at their last meeting.'

Baldwin chuckled boomingly. 'That accounts for it – that has to be my cousin on my father's side. Hartley M. – Stuffy citizen Hartley. I'll have to try to take the curse off the family name, now that I've met you, Captain.' He stuck out a huge hand. 'Gregory Baldwin, "Kettle Belly" to my friend. New and used helicopters is as close as I come to theoretical physics. *"Kettle Belly Baldwin, King of the Kopters"* – you must have seen my advertising.'

'Now that you mention it, I have.'

Baldwin pulled out a card. 'Here. If you ever need one, I'll give you a ten per cent off for knowing old Hartley.

20

Matter of fact, I can do right well by you in a year-old Curtiss, a family car without a mark on it.'

Gilead accepted the card and sat down. 'Not at the moment, thanks. You seem to have an odd sort of office, Mr. Baldwin.'

Baldwin chuckled again. 'In the course of a long life these things happen, Captain. I won't ask you why you are here or what you are doing in that monkey suit. Call me Kettle Belly.'

'Okay,' Gilead got up, and went to the door. Opposite the cell was a blank wall; there was no one in sight. He whistled and shouted – no answer.

'What's itching you, Captain?' Baldwin asked gently.

Gilead turned. His cellmate had dealt a solitaire hand on the bench and was calmly playing.

'I've got to raise the turnkey and send for a lawyer.'

'Don't fret about it. Let's play some cards.' He reached in a pocket. 'I've got a second deck; how about some Russian bank?'

'No, thanks. I've got to get out of here.' He shouted again – still no answer.

'Don't waste your lung power, Captain,' Baldwin advised him. 'They'll come when it suits them and not a second before. I *know*. Come play with me; it passes the time.' Baldwin appeared to be shuffling the two decks; Gilead could see that he was actually stacking the cards. The deception amused him; he decided to play – since the truth of Baldwin's advice was so evident.

'If you don't like Russian bank,' Kettle Belly went on, 'here is a game I learned as a kid.' He paused and stared into Gilead's eyes. 'It's instructive as well as entertaining, yet it's simple, once you catch on to it.' He started dealing out the cards. 'It makes a better game with two decks, because the black cards don't mean anything. Just the twenty-six red cards in each deck count – with the heart suit coming first. Each card scores according to its position in that sequence. The ace of hearts is one and

21

the king of hearts counts thirteen; the ace of diamonds is next at fourteen and so on. Savvy?'

'Yes.'

'And the blacks don't count. They're blanks . . . spaces. Ready to play?'

'What are the rules?'

'We'll deal out one hand for three; you'll learn faster as you see it. Then, when you've caught on, I'll play you for a half interest in the atomics trust – for ten bits in cash.' He resumed dealing, laying the cards out rapidly in columns, five to a row. He paused, finished. 'It's my deal, so it's your count. See what you get.'

It was evident that Baldwin's stacking had brought the red cards into groups, yet there was no evident advantage to it, nor was the count especially high – nor low. Gilead started at it, trying to figure out the man's game. The cheating, as cheating, seemed too bold to be probable.

Suddenly the cards jumped at him, arranged themselves in a meaningful array. He read:

```
XTHXY
CANXX
XXXSE
HEARX
XUSXX
```

The fact that there were only two fives-of-hearts available had affected the spelling but the meaning was clear. Gilead reached for the cards. 'I'll try one. I can beat that score.' He dipped into the tips belonging to the suit's owner. 'Ten bits it is.'

Baldwin covered it. Gilead shuffled, making even less attempt to cover up than had Baldwin. He dealt:

```
WHATS
XXXXX
XYOUR
GAMEX
XXXXX
```

Baldwin shoved the money towards him and anted again. 'Okay, my turn for revenge.' He laid out:

```
XXIMX
XONXX
YOURX
XXXXX
XSIDE
```

'I win again,' Gilead announced gleefully. 'Ante up.' He grabbed the cards and manipulated them:

```
YEAHX
PROVE
XXXXX
XXITX
XXXXX
```

Baldwin counted and said, 'You're too smart for me. Gimme the cards.' He produced another ten-bit piece and dealt again:

```
XXILX
HELPX
XXYOU
XGETX
OUTXX
```

'I should have cut the cards,' Gilead complained, pushing the money over. 'Let's double the bets.' Baldwin grunted and Gilead dealt again:

```
XNUTS
IMXXX
SAFER
XXINX
XGAOL
```

'I broke your luck,' Baldwin gloated. 'We'll double it again?'

```
                    XUXRX
                    XNUTS
                    THISX
                    NOXXX
                    XGAOL
```

The deal shifted:

```
                    KEEPX
                    XTALK
                    INGXX
                    XXXXX
                    XBUDX
```

Baldwin answered:

```
                    THISX
                    XXXXX
                    XXNEW
                    AGEXX
                    XHOTL
```

As he stacked the cards again Gilead considered these new factors. He was prepared to believe that he was hidden somewhere in the New Age Hotel; in fact the counterproposition that his opponents had permitted two ordinary cops to take him away to a normal city gaol was most unlikely – unless they had the gaol as fully under control as they quite evidently had the hotel. Nevertheless the point was not proven. As for Baldwin, he might be on Gilead's side; more probably he was planted as an *agent provocateur* – or he might be working for himself.

The permutations added up to six situations, only one of which made it desirable to accept Baldwin's offer for help in a gaol break – said situation being the least likely of the six.

Nevertheless, though he considered Baldwin a liar,

yet, he tentatively decided to accept. A static situation brought him no advantage; a dynamic situation – *any* dynamic situation – he might turn to his advantage. But more data were needed. 'These cards are sticky as candy,' he complained. 'You letting your money ride?'

'Suits.' Gilead dealt again:

```
XXXXX
WHYXX
AMXXX
XXXXI
XHERE
```

'You have the damnedest luck,' Baldwin commented:

```
FILMS
ESCAP
BEFORE
XUXXX
KRACK
```

Gilead swept up the cards, was about to 'shuffle,' when Baldwin said, 'Oh oh, school's out.' Footsteps could be heard in the passage. 'Good luck, boy,' Baldwin added.

Baldwin knew about the films, but had not used any of the dozen ways to identify himself as part of Gilead's own organisation. Therefore he was planted by the opposition, or he was a third factor.

More important, the fact that Baldwin knew about the films proved his assertion that this was not a gaol. It followed with bitter certainty that he, Gilead, stood no computable chance of getting out alive. The footsteps approaching the cell could be ticking off the last seconds of his life.

He knew now that he should have found means to report the destination of the films before going to the New Age. But Humpty Dumpty was off the wall, entropy always increases – but the films *must* be delivered.

The footsteps were quite close.

Baldwin might get out alive.

But who was Baldwin?

All the while he was 'shuffling' the cards. The action was not final; he had only to give them one true shuffle to destroy the message being set up in them. A spider settled from the ceiling, landed on the other man's hand. Baldwin, instead of knocking it off and crushing it, most carefully reached his arm out towards the wall and encouraged it to lower itself to the floor. 'Better stay out of the way, shorty,' he said gently, 'or one of the big boys is likely to step on you.'

The incident, small as it was, determined Gilead's decision – and with it, the fate of a planet. He stood up and handed the stacked deck to Baldwin. 'I owe you exactly ten-sixty,' he said carefully. 'Be sure to remember it – I'll see who our visitors are.'

The footstep had stopped outside the cell door.

There was two of them, dressed neither as police nor as guards; the masquerade was over. One stood well back, covering the manoeuvre with a Markheim, the other unlocked the door. 'Back against the wall, Fatso,' he ordered. 'Gilead, out you come. And take it easy, or, after we freeze you, I'll knock out your teeth just for fun.'

Baldwin shuffled back against the wall; Gilead came out slowly. He watched for any opening but the leader backed away from him without once getting between him and the man with the Markheim. 'Ahead of us and take it slow,' he was ordered. He complied, helpless under the precautions, unable to run, unable to fight.

Baldwin went back to the bench when they had gone. He dealt out the cards as if playing solitaire, swept them up again, and continued to deal himself solitaire hands. Presently he 'shuffled' the cards back to the exact order Gilead had left them and pocketed them.

The message had read: XTELLXFBSXPOBOXDE PTXXXCHI.

His two guards marched Gilead into a room and locked the door behind him, leaving themselves outside. He found himself in a large window overlooking the city and a reach of the river; balancing it on the left hung a solid portraying a lunar landscape in convincing colour and depth. In front of him was a rich but not ostentatious executive desk.

The lower part of his mind took in these details; his attention could be centred only on the person who sat at that desk. She was old but not senile, frail but not helpless. Her eyes were very much alive, her expression serene. Her translucent, well-groomed hands were busy with a frame of embroidery.

On the desk in front of her were two pneumo mailing tubes, a pair of slippers, and some tattered, soiled remnants of cloth and plastic.

She looked up. 'How do you do, Captain Gilead?' she said in a thin, sweet soprano suitable for singing hymns.

Gilead bowed. 'Well, thank you – and you, Mrs. Keithley?'

'You know me, I see.'

'Madame would be famous if only for her charities.'

'You are kind. Captain, I will not waste your time. I had hoped that we could release you without fuss, but –' She indicated the two tubes in front of her. '– you can see for yourself that we must deal with you further.'

So?'

'Come, now, Captain. You mailed *three* tubes. These two are only dummies, and the third did not reach its apparent destination. It is possible that it was badly addressed and has been rejected by the sorting machines. If so, we shall have it in due course. But it seems much more likely that you found some way to change its address – likely to the point of pragmatic certainty.'

'Or possibly I corrupted your servant.'

She shook her head slightly. 'We examined him quite thoroughly before –'

'Before he died?'

'Please, Captain, let's not change the subject. I must

27

know where you sent that other tube. You cannot be hypnotised by ordinary means; you have an acquired immunity to hypnotic drugs. Your tolerance for pain extends beyond the threshold of unconsciousness. All of these things have already been proved, else you would not be in the job you are in; I shall not put either of us to the inconvenience of proving them again. Yet I must have that tube. What is your price?'

'You assume that I have a price.'

She smiled. 'If the old saw has any exceptions, history does not record them. Be reasonable, Captain. Despite your admitted immunity to ordinary forms of examination, there are ways of breaking down – of *changing* – a man's character so that he becomes really quite pliant under examination . . . ways that we learned from the commissars. But those ways take time and a woman my age has no time to waste.'

Gilead lied convincingly. 'It's not your age, ma'am; it is the fact that you know that you must obtain that tube at once or you will never get it.' He was hoping – more than that, he was *willing* – that Baldwin would have sense enough to examine the cards for one last message . . . and act on it. If Baldwin failed and he, Gilead, died, the tube would eventually come to rest in a dead-letter office and would in time be destroyed.

'You are probably right. Nevertheless, Captain, I will go ahead with the Mindszenty technique if you insist upon it. What do you say to ten million plutonium credits?'

Gilead believed her first statement. He reviewed in his mind the means by which a man bound hand and foot, or worse, could kill himself unassisted. 'Ten million plutons and a knife in my back?' he answered. 'Let's be practical.'

'Convincing assurance would be given before you need talk.'

'Even so, it is not my price. After all, you are worth at least five hundred million plutons.'

28

She leaned forward. 'I like you, Captain. You are a man of strength. I am an old woman, without heirs. Suppose you became my partner – and my successor?'

'Pie in the sky.'

'No, no! I mean it. My age and sex do not permit me actively to serve myself; I must rely on others. Captain, I am very tired of inefficient tools, of men who can let things be spirited away right from under their noses. Imagine!' She made a little gesture of exasperation, clutching her hand into a claw. 'You and I could go far, Captain. I need you.'

'But I do not need you, madame. And I won't have you.'

She made no answer, but touched a control on her desk. A door on the left dilated; two men and a girl came in. The girl Gilead recognised as the waitress from the Grand Concourse Drug Store. They had stripped her bare, which seemed to him an unnecessary indignity since her working uniform could not possibly have concealed a weapon.

The girl, once inside, promptly blew her top, protesting, screaming, using language unusual to her age and sex – an hysterical thalamic outburst of volcanic proportions.

'Quiet, child!'

The girl stopped in midstream, looked with surprise at Mrs. Keithley, and shut up. Nor did she start again, but stood there, looking even younger than she was and somewhat aware of and put off stride by her nakedness. She was covered now with goose flesh, one tear cut a white line down her dust-smeared face, stopped at her lip. She licked at it and sniffled.

'You were out of observation once, Captain,' Mrs. Keithley went on, 'during which time this person saw you twice. Therefore we will examine her.'

Gilead shook his head. 'She knows no more than a goldfish. But go ahead – five minutes of hypno will convince you.'

'Oh, no, Captain! Hypno is sometimes fallible; if she is a member of your bureau, it is certain to be fallible.'

She signalled to one of the men attending the girl; he went to a cupboard and opened it. 'I am old-fashioned,' the old woman went on. 'I trust simple mechanical means much more than I do the cleverest of clinical procedures.'

Gilead saw the implements that the man was removing from the cupboard and started forward. 'Stop that!' he commanded. 'You can't do that –'

He bumped his nose quite hard.

The man paid him no attention. Mrs. Keithley said, 'Forgive me, Captain. I should have told you that this room is not one room, but two. T ıe partition is merely glass, but very special glass – I use the room for difficult interviews. There is no need to hurt yourself by trying to reach us.'

'Just a moment!'

'Yes, Captain?'

'Your time is already running out. Let the girl and me go free *now*. You are aware that there are several hundred men searching this city for me even now – and that they will not stop until they have taken it apart panel by panel.'

'I think not. A man answering your description to the last factor caught the South African rocket twenty minutes after you registered at the New Age Hotel. He was carrying your very own identifications. He will not reach South Africa, but the manner of his disappearance will point to desertion rather than accident or suicide.'

Gilead dropped the matter. 'What do you plan to gain by abusing this child? You have all she knows; certainly you do not believe that we could afford to trust in such as she?'

Mrs. Keithley pursed her lips. 'Frankly, I do not expect to learn anything from her. I may learn something from you.'

'I see.'

The leader of the two men looked questioningly at his mistress; she motioned him to go ahead. The girl stared blankly at him, plainly unaware of the uses of the equipment he had gotten out. He and his partner got busy.

Shortly the girl screamed, continued to scream for a few moments in a high ululation. Then it stopped as she fainted.

They roused her and stood her up again. She stood, swaying and staring stupidly at her poor hands, forever damaged even for the futile purposes to which she had been capable of putting them. Blood spread down her wrists and dripped on a plastic tarpaulin, placed there earlier by the second of the two men.

Gilead did nothing and said nothing. Knowing as he did that the tube he was protecting contained matters measured in millions of lives, the problem of the girl, as a problem, did not even arise. It disturbed a deep and very ancient part of his brain, but almost automatically he cut that part off and lived for the time in his fore-brain.

Consciously he memorised the faces, skulls and figures of the two men and filed the data under 'personal.' Thereafter he unobstrusively gave his attention to the scene out the window. He had been noting it all through the interview but he wanted to give it explicit thought. He recast what he saw in terms of what it would look like had he been able to look squarely out the window and decided that he was on the ninety-first floor of the New Age Hotel and approximately one hundred and thirty metres from the north end. He filed this under 'professional.'

When the girl died, Mrs. Keithley left the room without speaking to him. The men gathered up what was left in the tarpaulin and followed her. Presently the two guards returned and, using the same foolproof methods, took him back to his cell.

As soon as the guards had gone and Kettle Belly was free to leave his position against the wall, he came forward and pounded Gilead on the shoulders. 'Hi, boy! I'm sure glad to see you – I was scared I would never lay eyes

31

on you again. How was it? Pretty rough?'

'No, they didn't hurt me; they just asked some questions.'

'You're lucky. Some of of those crazy damn cops play mean when they get you alone in a back room. Did they let you call your lawyer?'

'No.'

'They ain't through with you. You want to watch it, kid.'

Gilead sat down on the bench. 'The hell with them. Want to play some more cards?'

'Don't mind if I do. I feel lucky.' Baldwin pulled out the double deck, riffled through it. Gilead took them and did the same. Good! they were in the order he had left them in. He ran his thumb across the edges again – yes, even the black nulls were unchanged in sequence; apparently Kettle Belly had simply stuck them in his pocket without examining them, without suspecting that a last message had been written in to them. He felt sure that Baldwin would not have left the message set up if he had read it. Since he found himself still alive, he was much relieved to think this.

He gave the cards one true shuffle, then started stacking them. His first lay-out read:

XXXXX
ESCAP
XXATX
XXXXX
XONCE

'Gotcha that time!' Baldwin crowed. 'Ante up.'

DIDXX
XYOUX
XXXXX
XXXXX
CRACK

32

'Let it ride,' announced Gilead and took the deal;

```
XXNOX
BUTXX
XXXXX
XLETS
XXGOX
```

'You're too derned lucky to live,' complained Baldwin. 'Look – we'll leave the bets doubled and double the lay-out. I want a fair chance to get my money back.'

His next lay-out read:

```
XXXXX
XTHXN
XXXXX
THXYX
NEEDX
XXUXX
ALIVX
XXXXX
PLAYX
XXXUP
```

'Didn't do you much good, did it?' Gilead commented, took the cards and started arranging them.

'There's something mighty funny about a man that wins all the time,' Baldwin grumbled. He watched Gilead narrowly. Suddenly his hand shot out, grabbed Gilead's wrist. 'I thought so,' he yelled. A goddam card sharp –' Gilead shook his hand off. 'Why, you obscene fat slug!'

'Caught you! *Caught you!*' Kettle Belly reclaimed his hold, grabbed the other wrist as well. They struggled and rolled to the floor.

Gilead discovered two things: this awkward, bulgy man was an artist at every form of dirty fighting and he could simulate it convincingly without damaging his partner. His nerve holds were an inch off the nerve; his kneeings were to thigh muscle rather than to the crotch.

Baldwin tried for a chancery strangle; Gilead let him

take it. The big man settled the flat of his forearm against the point of Gilead's chin rather than against his Adam's apple and proceeded to 'strangle' him.

There were running footsteps in the corridor.

Gilead caught a glimpse of the guards as they reached the door. They stopped momentarily; the bell of the Markheim was too big to use through the steel grating, the charge would be screened and grounded. Apparently they did not have pacifier bombs with them, for they hesitated. Then the leader quickly unlocked the door, while the man with the Markheim dropped back to the cover position.

Baldwin ignored them, while continuing his stream of profanity and abuse at Gilead. He let the first man almost reach them before he suddenly said in Gilead's ear, 'Close your eyes!' At which he broke just as suddenly.

Gilead sensed an incredibly dazzling flash of light even through his eyelids. Almost on top of it he heard a muffled crack; he opened his eyes and saw that the first man was down, his head twisted at a grotesque angle.

The man with the Markheim was shaking his head; the muzzle of his weapon weaved around. Baldwin was charging him in a waddle, back and knees bent until he was hardly three feet tall. The blinded guard could hear him, let fly a charge in the direction of the noise; it passed over Baldwin.

Baldwin was on him; the two went down. There was another cracking noise of ruptured bone and another dead man. Baldwin stood up, grasping the Markheim, keeping it pointed down the corridor. 'How are your eyes, kid?' he called out anxiously.

'They're all right.'

'Then come take this chiller.' Gilead moved up, took the Markheim. Baldwin ran to the dead end of the corridor where a window looked out over the city. The window did not open; there was no 'copter step' beyond it. It was merely a straight drop. He came running back.

Gilead was shuffling possibilities in his mind. Events

34

had moved by Baldwin's plan, not by his. As a result of his visit to Mrs. Keithley's 'interview room' he was oriented in space. The corridor ahead and a turn to the left should bring him to the quick-drop shaft. Once in the basement and armed with a Markheim, he felt sure that he could fight his way out – with Baldwin in trail if the man would follow. If not – well, there was too much at stake.

Baldwin was into the cell and out again almost at once. 'Come along!' Gilead snapped. A head showed at the bend in the corridor; he let fly at it and the owner of the head passed out on the floor.

'Out of my way, kid!' Baldwin answered. He was carrying the heavy bench on which they had 'played' cards. He started up the corridor with it, toward the sealed window, gaining speed remarkably as he went.

His makeshift battering ram struck the window heavily. The plastic bulged, ruptured, and snapped like a soap bubble. The bench went on through, disappeared from sight, while Baldwin teetered on hands and knees, a thousand feet of nothingness under his chin.

'Kid!' he yelled. 'Close in! Fall back!'

Gilead backed towards him, firing twice more as he did so. He still did not see how Baldwin planned to get out, but the big man had demonstrated that he had resourcefulness – and resources.

Baldwin was whistling through his fingers and waving. In violation of all city traffic rules a helicopter separated itself from the late afternoon throng, cut through a lane and approached the window. It hovered just far enough away to keep from fouling its blades. The driver opened the door, a line snaked across and Kettle Belly caught it. With great speed he made it fast to the window's polariser knob, then grabbed the Markheim. 'You first,' he snapped. 'Hurry!'

Gilead dropped to his knees and grasped the line; the driver immediately increased his tip speed and tilted his rotor; the line tautened. Gilead let it take his weight, then swarmed across it. The driver gave him a hand up while controlling his craft like a highschool horse with his other hand.

The 'copter bucked; Gilead turned and saw Baldwin coming across, a fat spider on a web. As he himself helped the big man in, the driver reached down and cut the line. The ship bucked again and slid away.

There were already men standing in the broken window. 'Get lost, Steve!' Baldwin ordered. The driver gave his tip jets another notch and tilted the rotor still more; the 'copter swooped away. He eased it into the traffic stream and inquired, 'Where to?'

'Set her for home – and tell the other boys to go home, too. No – you've got your hands full; I'll tell them!' Baldwin crowded up into the other pilot's seat, slipped phones and settled a quiet-mike over his mouth. The driver adjusted his car to the traffic, set up a combination on his pilot, then settled back and opened a picture magazine.

Shortly Baldwin took off the phones and came back to the passenger compartment. 'Takes a lot of 'copters to be sure you have one cruising by when you need it,' he said conversationally. 'Fortunately, I've got a lot of 'em. Oh, by the way, this is Steve Halliday. Steven, meet Joe – Joe, what *is* your last name?'

'Greene,' answered Gilead.

'Howdy,' said the driver, and let his eyes go back to his magazine.

Gilead considered the situation. He was not sure that it had been improved. Kettle Belly, whatever he was, was more than a used 'copter dealer – *and* he knew about the films. This boy Steve looked like a harmless young extrovert but, then Kettle Belly himself looked like a lunk. He considered trying to overpower both of them, remembered Kettle Belly's virtuosity in rough-and-tumble fighting, and decided against it. Perhaps Kettle Belly really was on his side, completely and utterly. He heard rumours that the department used more than one echelon of operatives and he had no way of being sure that he himself

36

was at the top level.

'Kettle Belly,' he went on, 'could you set me down at the airport first? I'm in one hell of a hurry.'

Baldwin looked him over. 'Sure, if you say so. But I thought you would want to swap those duds? You're as conspicuous as a preacher at a stag party. And how are you fixed for cash?'

With his fingers Gilead counted the change that had come with the suit. A man without cash had one arm in a sling. 'How long would it take?'

'Ten minutes extra, maybe.'

Gilead thought again about Kettle Belly's fighting ability and decided that there was no way for a fish in water to get any wetter. 'Okay.' He settled back and relaxed completely.

Presently he turned again to Baldwin. 'By the way, how did you manage to sneak in that dazzle bomb?'

Kettle Belly chuckled. 'I'm a large man, Joe; there's an awful lot of me to search.' He laughed again. 'You'd be amazed at where I had that hidden.'

Gilead changed the subject. 'How did you happen to be there in the first place?'

Baldwin sobered. 'That's a long and complicated story. Come back some day when you're not in such a rush and I'll tell you all about it.'

'I'll do that – soon.'

'Good. Maybe I can sell you that used Curtiss at the same time.'

The pilot alarm sounded; the driver put down his magazine and settled the craft on the roof of Baldwin's establishment.

Baldwin was as good as his word. He took Gilead to his office, sent for clothes – which showed up with great speed – and handed Gilead a wad of bills suitable to stuff a pillow. 'You can mail it back,' he said.

'I'll bring it back in person,' promised Gilead.

'Good. Be careful out on the street. Some of our friends

are sure to be around.'

'I'll be careful.' He left, as casually as if he had called there on business, but feeling less sure of himself than usual. Baldwin himself remained a mystery and, in his business, Gilead could not afford mysteries.

There was a public phone booth in the lobby of Baldwin's building. Gilead went in, scrambled, then coded a different relay station from the one he had attempted to use before. He gave his booth's code and instructed the operator to scramble back. In a matter of minutes he was talking to his chief in New Washington.

'Joe! Where the hell have you been?'

'Later, boss – get this.' In departmental oral code, as an added precaution, he told his chief that the films were in post office box 1060, Chicago, and insisted that they be picked up by a major force at once.

His chief turned away from the view plate, then returned, 'Okay, it's done. Now what happened to you?'

'Later, boss, later. I think I've got some friends outside who are anxious to rassle with me. Keep me here and I may get a hole in my head.'

'Okay – but head right back here. I want a full report; I'll wait here for you.'

'Right.' He switched off.

He left the booth lightheartedly, with the feeling of satisfaction that comes from a hard job successfully finished. He rather hoped that some of his 'friends' would show up; he felt like kicking somebody who needed kicking.

But they disappointed him. He boarded the transcontinental rocket without alarms and slept all the way to New Washington.

He reached the Federal Bureau of Security by one of many concealed routes and went to his boss's office. After scan and voice check he was let in. Bonn looked up and scowled.

Gilead ignored the expression; Bonn usually scowled. 'Agent Joseph Briggs, three-four-oh-nine-seven-two, reporting back from assignment, sir,' he said evenly.

Bonn switched a desk control to 'recording' and another to 'covert.' 'You are, eh? Why, thumb-fingered idiot! how do you dare to show your face around here?'

'Easy now, boss – what's the trouble?'

Bonn fumed incoherently for a time, then said, 'Briggs, twelve star men covered that pick-up – and the box was empty. Post office box ten-sixty, Chicago, indeed! Where are those films? Was it a cover up? Have you got them with you?'

Gilead-Briggs restrained his surprise. 'No. I mailed them at the Grand Concourse post office to the address you just named.' He added, 'The machine may have kicked them out; I was forced to letter by hand the machine symbols.'

Bonn looked suddenly hopeful. He touched another control and said, 'Carruthers! On that Briggs matter: Check the rejection stations for that routing.' He thought and then added, then try a rejection sequence on the assumption that the first symbol was acceptable to the machine but mistaken. Also for each of the other symbols; run them simultaneously – crash priority for all agents and staff. After that try combinations of symbols taken two at a time, then three at a time, and so on.' He switched off.

'The total of that series you just set up is every postal address in the continent,' Briggs suggested mildly. 'It can't be done.'

'It's got to be done! Man, have you any idea of the importance of those films you were guarding?'

'Yes. The director at Moon Base told me what I was carrying.'

'You don't act as if you did. You've lost the most valuable thing this or any other government can possess – the absolute weapon. Yet you stand there blinking at me as if you had mislaid a pack of cigarettes.'

'Weapon?' objected Briggs. I wouldn't call the nova effect that, unless you class suicide as a weapon. And I don't concede that I've lost it. As an agent acting alone and charged primarily with keeping it out of the hands of others, I used the best means available in an emergency to protect it. That is well within the limits of my authority. I was spotted, by some means –'

'You shouldn't have been spotted!'

'Granted. But I was. I was unsupported and my estimate of the situation did not include a probability of staying alive. Therefore I had to protect my charge by some means which did not depend on my staying alive.'

'But you *did* stay alive – you're here.'

'Not my doing nor yours, I assure you. I should have been covered. It was your order, you will remember, that I act alone.'

Bonn looked sullen. 'That was necessary.'

'So? In any case I don't see what all the shooting is about. Either the films show up, or they are lost and will be destroyed as unclaimed mail. So I go back to the Moon and get another set of prints.'

'Why not?'

Bonn hesitated a long time. 'There were just two sets. You had the originals, which were to be placed in a vault in the Archives – and the others were to be destroyed at once when the originals were known to be secure.'

'Yes? What's the hitch?

'You don't see the importance of the procedure. Every working paper, every file, every record was destroyed when these films were made. Every technician, every assistant, received hypno. The intention was not only to protect the results of the research, but to wipe out the very fact that the research had taken place. There aren't a dozen people in the system who even know of the existence of the nova effect.'

Briggs had his own opinions on this point, based on recent experience, but he kept still about them. Bonn went on, 'The Secretary has been after me steadily to let him know when the originals were secured. He has been quite insistent, quite critical. When you called in, I told him that the films were safe and that he would have them in a few minutes.'

'Well?'

'Don't you see, you fool – he gave the order at once to destroy the other copies.'

Briggs whistled. 'Jumped the gun, didn't he?'

'That's not the way he'll figure it – mind you, the President was pressuring *him*. He'll say that *I* jumped the gun.'

'And so you did.'

'No, you jumped the gun. You told me the films were in that box.'

'Hardly. I said I had sent them there.'

'No, you didn't.'

'Get out the tape and play it back.'

'There is no tape – by the President's own order no records are kept on this operation.'

'So? Then why are you recording now?'

'Because,' Bonn answered sharply, 'someone is going to pay for this and it is not going to be me.'

'Meaning,' Briggs said slowly, 'that it is going to be me.'

'I didn't say that. It might be the Secretary.'

'If his head rolls, so will yours. No, both of you are figuring on using me. Before you plan on that, hadn't you better hear my report? It might affect your plans. I've got news for you, boss.'

Bonn drummed the desk. 'Go ahead. It had better be good.'

In a passionless monotone Briggs recited all events as recorded by sharp memory from receipt of the films on the Moon to the present moment. Bonn listened impatiently.

Finished, Briggs waited. Bonn got up and strode around the room. Finally he stopped and said, 'Briggs, I never heard such a fantastic pack of lies in my life. A fat man who plays cards! A wallet that wasn't your wallet – your clothes stolen! And Mrs. Keithley – Mrs. *Keith-*

ley! Don't you know that she is one of the strongest supporters of the Administration?'

Briggs said nothing. Bonn went on, 'Now I'll tell you what actually did happen. Up to the time you grounded.'

'How do you know?'

'Because you were covered, naturally. You don't think I would trust this to one man, do you?'

'Why didn't you tell me? I could have hollered for help and saved all this.'

Bonn brushed it aside. 'You engaged a runner, dismissed him, went in that drugstore, came out and went to the post office. There was no fight in the concourse for the simple reason that no one was following you. At the post office you mailed three tubes, one of which may or may not have contained the films. You went from there to the New Age Hotel, left it twenty minutes later and caught the transrocket for Cape Town. You –'

'Just a moment,' objected Briggs. 'How could I have done that and still be here now?'

'Eh?' For a moment Bonn seemed stumped. 'That's just a detail; you were positively identified. For that matter, it would have been a far, far better thing for you if you had stayed on that rocket. In fact –' The bureau chief got a faraway look in his eyes. '– you'll be better off for the time being if we assume officially that you did stay on that rocket. You are in a bad spot, Briggs, a very bad spot. You did not muff this assignment – you sold out! '

Briggs looks at him levelly. 'You are preferring charges?'

'Not just now. That is why it is best to assume that you stayed on that rocket – until matters settle down, clarify.'

Briggs did not need a graph to show him what solution would come out when 'matters clarified.' He took from a pocket a memo pad, scribbled on it briefly, and handed it to Bonn.

It read: 'I resign my appointment effective immediately.' He had added signature, thumbprint, date and hour.

'So long, boss,' he added. He turned slightly, as if to go.

Bonn yelled, 'Stop! Briggs, you are under arrest.' He reached towards his desk.

Briggs cuffed him in the windpipe, added one to the pit of Bonn's stomach. He slowed down then and carefully made sure that Bonn would remain out for a satisfactory period. Examination of Bonn's desk produced a knockout kit; he added a two-hour hypodermic, placing it inconspicuously beside a mole near the man's backbone. He wiped the needle, restored everything to its proper place, removed the current record from the desk and wiped the tape of all mention of himself, including door check. He left the desk set to 'covert' and 'do not disturb' and left by another of the concealed routes to the Bureau.

He went to the rocket port, bought a ticket, unreserved, for the first ship to Chicago. There was twenty minutes to wait; he made a couple of minor purchases from clerks rather than from machines, letting his face be seen. When the Chicago ship was called he crowded forward with the rest.

At the inner gate, just short of the weighing-in platform, he became part of the crowd present to see passengers off, rather than a passenger himself. He waved at someone in the line leaving the weighing station beyond the gate, smiled, called out a goodbye, and let the crowd carry him back from the gate as it closed. He peeled off from the crowd at the men's washroom. When he came out there were several hasty but effective changes in his appearance.

More important, his manner was different.

A short, illicit transaction in a saloon near a hiring hall provided the work card he needed; fifty-five minutes later he was headed acrosss country as Jack Gillespie, loader and helper-driver on a diesel freighter.

Could his addressing of the pneumo tube have been bad enough to cause the automatic postal machines to reject it? He let the picture of the label, as it had been when he had completed it, build in his mind until it was as sharp as the countryside flowing past him. No, his lettering of the symbols had been perfect and correct; the machines would accept it.

Could the machine have kicked out the tube for another cause, say a turned up edge of the gummed label? Yes, but the written label was sufficient to enable a postal clerk to get it back in the groove. One such delay did not exceed ten minutes, even during the rush hour. Even with five such delays the tube would have reached Chicago more than one hour before he reported to Bonn by phone.

Suppose the gummed label had peeled off entirely; in such case the tube would have gone to the same destination as the two cover-up tubes.

In which case Mrs. Keithley would have gotten it, since she had been able to intercept or receive the other two.

Therefore the tube had reached the Chicago post office box.

Therefore Kettle Belly *had* read the message in the stacked cards, had given instruction to someone in Chicago, had done so while at the helicopter's radio. After an event, 'possible' and 'true' are equivalent ideas, whereas 'probable' becomes a measure of one's ignorance. To call a conclusion 'improbable' *after the event* was self-confusing amphigory.

Therefore Kettle Belly Baldwin had the films – a conclusion he had reached in Bonn's office.

Two hundred miles from New Washington he worked up an argument with the top driver and got himself fired. From a local booth in the town where he was dropped he scrambled through to Baldwin's business office. 'Tell him I'm a man who owes him money.'

Shortly the big man's face built up on the screen. 'Hi, kid! How's tricks?'

44

'I'm fired.'

'I thought you would be.'

'Worse than that – I'm wanted.'

'Naturally.'

'I'd like to talk with you.'

'Swell. Where are you?'

Gilead told him.

'You're clean?'

'For a few hours, at least.'

'Go to the local airport. Steve will pick you up.'

Steve did so, nodded a greeting, jumped his craft into the air, set his pilot, and went back to his reading. When the ship settled down on course, Gilead noted it and asked, 'Where are we going?'

'The boss's ranch. Didn't he tell you?'

'No.' Gilead knew it was possible that he was being taken for a one way ride. True, Baldwin had enabled him to escape an otherwise pragmatically certain death – it was certain that Mrs Keithley had not intended to let him stay alive longer than suited her uses, else she would not have had the girl killed in his presence. Until he had arrived at Bonn's office, he had assumed that Baldwin had saved him because he knew something that Baldwin most urgently wanted to know – whereas now it looked as if Baldwin had saved him for altruistic reasons.

Gilead conceded the existence in this world of altruistic reasons, but was inclined not to treat them as 'least hypothesis' until all other possible hypotheses had been eliminated; Baldwin might have had his own reasons for wishing him to live long enough to report to New Washington and nevertheless be pleased to wipe him out now that he was a wanted man whose demise would cause no comment.

Baldwin might even be a partner in these dark matters of Mrs. Keithley. In some ways that was the simplest explanation though it left other factors unexplained. In any case Baldwin was a key actor – and he had the films. The risk was necessary.

Gilead did not worry about it. The factors known to

him were chalked up on the blackboard of his mind, there to remain until enough variables become constants to permit a solution by logic. The ride was very pleasant.

Steve put him down on the lawn of a large rambling ranch house, introduced him to a motherly old party named Mrs. Garver, and took off. 'Make yourself at home, Joe,' she told him. 'Your room is the last one in the east wing – shower across from it. Supper in ten minutes.'

He thanked her and took the suggestion, getting back to the living room with a minute or two to spare. Several others, a dozen or more of both sexes, were there. The place seemed to be a sort of a dude ranch – not entirely dude, as he had seen Herefords on the spread as Steve and he were landing.

The other guests seemed to take his arrival as a matter of course. No one asked why he was there. One of the women introduced herself as Thalia Wagner and then took him around the group. Ma Garver came in swinging a dinner bell as this was going on and they all filed into a long, low dining froom. Gilead could not remember when he had had so good a meal in such amusing company.

After eleven hours of sleep, his first real rest in several days, came fully, suddenly awake at a group of sounds his subconscious could not immediately classify and refused to discount. He opened his eyes, swept the room with them, and was at once out of bed, crouching on the side away from the door.

There were hurrying footsteps moving past the bedroom door. There were two voices, one male, one female, outside the door; the female was Thalia Wagner, the man he could not place.

Male: 'tsumaeq?'
Female: 'no!'
Male: 'zulntisi.'
Female: 'ipbit' New Jersey.'

46

These are not precisely the sounds that Gilead heard, first because of the limitations of phonetic symbols, and second because his ears were not used to the sounds. Hearing is a function of the brain, not of the ear; his brain, sophisticated as it was, nevertheless insisted on forcing the sounds that reached his ears into familiar pockets rather than to stop to create new ones.

Thalia Wagner identified, he relaxed and stood up. Thalia was part of the unknown situation he accepted in coming here; a stranger known to her he must accept also. The new unknowns, including the odd language, he filed under 'pending' and put aside.

The clothes he had had were gone, but his money – Baldwin's money, rather – was where his clothes had been and with it his work card as Jack Gillespie and his few personal articles. By them some one had laid out a fresh pair of walking shorts and new sneakers, in his size.

He noted, with almost shocking surprise, that someone had been able to serve him thus without waking him.

He put on his shorts and shoes and went out. Thalia and her companion had left while he dressed. No one was about and he found the dining room empty, but three places were set, including his own of supper, and hot dishes and facilities were on the side board. He selected baked ham and hot rolls, fried four eggs, poured coffee. Twenty minutes later, warmly replenished, and still alone, he stepped out on the veranda.

It was a beautiful day. He was drinking it in and eyeing with friendly interest a desert lark when a young woman came around the side of the house. She was dressed much as he was, allowing for difference in sex, and she was comely, though not annoyingly so. 'Good morning,' he said.

She stopped, put her hands on her hips, and looked him up and down. 'Well! ' she said. 'Why doesn't somebody tell me these things?'

Then she added, 'Are you married?'

'No.'

'I'm shopping around. Object: matrimony. Let's get acquainted.'

'I'm a hard man to marry. I've been avoiding it for years.'

'They're all hard to marry,' she said bitterly. 'there's a new colt down at the corral. Come on.'

They went. The colt's name was War Conqueror of Baldwin; hers was Gail. After proper protocol with mare and son they left. 'Unless you have pressing engagements,' said Gail, 'now is a salubrious time to go swimming.'

'If salubrious means what I think it does, yes.'

The spot was shaded by cottonwoods, the bottom was sandy; for a while he felt like a boy again, with all such matters as lies and nova effects and death and violence away in some improbable, remote dimension. After a long while he pulled himself up on the bank and said, 'Gail, what does "tsumaeq" mean?'

'Come again?' she answered. 'I had water in my ear.'

He repeated all of the conversation he had heard. She looked incredulous, then laughed. 'You didn't hear that, Joe, you just didn't.' She added, 'You got the "New Jersey" part right.'

'But I did.'

'Say it again.'

He did so, more carefully, and giving a fair imitation of the speakers' accents.

Gail chortled. 'I got the gist of it that time. That Thalia; some day some strong man is going to wring her neck.'

'But what does it mean?'

Gail gave him a long, sidewise look. 'If you ever find out, I really will marry you, in spite of your protests.'

Someone was whistling from the hilltop. 'Joe! Joe Greene – the boss wants you.'

'Gotta go,' he said to Gail. 'G'bye.'

'See you later,' she corrected him.

Baldwin was waiting in a study as comfortable as himself. 'Hi, Joe,' he greeted him. 'Grab a seatful of chair. They been treating you right?'

'Yes, indeed. Do you always set as good a table as I've enjoyed so far?'

Baldwin patted his middle. 'How do you think I came by my nickname?'

'Kettle Belly, I'd like a lot of explanations.'

'Joe, I'm right sorry you lost your job. If I'd had my druthers, it wouldn't have been the way it was.'

'Are you working with Mrs. Keithley?'

'No. I'm against her.'

'I'd like to believe that, but I've no reason to – yet. What were you doing where I found you?'

'They had grabbed me – Mrs. Keithley and her boys.'

'They just happened to grab you – and just happened to stuff you in the same cell with me – and you just happened to know about the films I was supposed to be guarding – and you just happened to have a double deck of cards in your pocket? Now, really! '

'If I hadn't had the cards, we would have found some other way to talk,' Kettle Belly said mildly. 'Wouldn't we, now?'

'Yes. Granted.'

'I didn't mean to suggest that the set up was an accident. We had you covered from Moon Base; when you were grabbed – or rather as soon as you let them suck you into the New Age, I saw to it that they grabbed me too; I figured I might have a chance to lend you a hand, once I was inside.' He added, 'I kinda let them think I was an FBS man, too.'

'I see. Then it was just luck that they locked us up together.'

'Not luck,' Kettle Belly objected. 'Luck is a bonus that follows careful planning – it's never free. There was a computable probability that they would put us together in hopes of finding out what they wanted to know. We hit the jackpot because we paid for the chance. If we hadn't, I would have had to crush out of that cell and look for you – but I had to be inside to do it.'

'Who is Mrs. Keithley?'

'Other than what she is publicly, I take it. She is the queen bee – or the black widow – of a gang. "Gang" is a poor word – power group, maybe. One of several such groups, more or less tied together where their interests don't cross. Between them they divvy up the country for whatever they want like two cats splitting a gopher.'

Gilead nodded; he knew what Baldwin meant, though he had not known that the enormously respected Mrs. Keithley was in such matters – not until his nose had been rubbed in the fact. 'And what are you, Kettle Belly?'

'Now, Joe – I like you and I'm truly sorry you're in a jam. You led wrong a couple of times and I wa⁀ obliged to trump, as the stakes were high. See here. I feel that I owe you something; what do you say to this; we'll fix you up with a brand-new personality, vacuum tight – even new finger prints if you want them. Pick any spot on the globe you like and any occupation; we'll supply all the money you need to start over – or money enough to re-tire and play with the cuties the rest of your life. What do you say?'

'No.' There was no hesitation.

'You've no close relatives, no intimate friends. Think about it, I can't put you back in your job, this is the best I can do.'

'I've thought about it. The de⁀il with the job, I want to finish my case! you're the key to it.'

'Reconsider, Joe. This is your chance to get out of affairs of state and lead a normal, happy life.'

' "Happy," he says! '

'Well, safe, anyhow. If you insist on going further your life expectancy becomes extremely problematical.'

'I don't recall ever having tried to play safe.'

'You're the doctor, Joe. In that case –' A speaker on Baldwin's desk uttered: 'œn e ʀ hog rylp.

Baldwin answered, 'nu,' and sauntered quickly to the

fireplace. An early-morning fire still smouldered in it. He grasped the mantelpiece, pulled it towards him. The entire masonry assembly, hearth, mantel and grate came towards him, leaving an arch in the wall. 'Duck down stairs, Joe,' he said. 'It's a raid.'

'A real priest's hole!'

'Yeah, corny, ain't it? This joint has more bolt holes than a rabbit's nest – and booby-trapped, too. Too many gadgets, if you ask me.' He went back to his desk, opened a drawer, removed three film spools and dropped them in a pocket.

Gilead was about to go down the staircase; seeing the spool, he stopped. 'Go ahead, Joe,' Baldwin said urgently. 'You're covered and outnumbered. With this raid showing up we wouldn't have time to fiddle, we'd just have to kill you.'

They stopped in a room well underground, another study much like the one above, though lacking sunlight and view. Baldwin said something in the odd language to the mike on the desk, and was answered. Gilead experimented with the idea that the lingo might be reversed English, discarded the notion.

'As I was saying,' Baldwin went on, 'if you are dead set on knowing all the answers –'

'Just a moment. What about this raid?'

'Just the government boys. They won't be rough and not too thorough. Ma Garver can handle them. We won't have to hurt anybody as long as they don't use penetration radar.'

Gilead smiled wryly at the disparagement of his own former service. 'And if they do?'

'That gimmick over there squeals like a pig if it's touched by penetration frequencies. Even then we're safe against anything short of an A-bomb. They won't do that! they want the films, not a hole in the ground. Which reminds me – here, catch.'

Gilead found himself suddenly in possession of the films which were at the root of the matter. He unspooled a few frames and made certain that they were indeed the right films. He sat still and considered how he might get off his limb and back to the ground without dropping the eggs. The speaker again uttered something; Baldwin did not answer it but said, 'We won't be down here long.'

'Bonn seems to have decided to check my report.' Some of his – former – comrades were upstairs. If he did let Baldwin in, could he locate the inside control for the door?

'Bonn is a poor sort. He'll check me – but not too thoroughly; I'm rich. He won't check Mrs. Keithley at all; she's too rich. He thinks with his political ambitions instead of his head. His late predecessor was a better man – he was one of us.'

Gilead's tentative plans underwent an abrupt reversal. His oath had been to a government; his personal loyalty had been given to his former boss. 'Prove that last remark and I shall be much interested.'

'No, you'll come to learn that it's true – if you still insist on knowing the answers. Through checking those films, Joe? Toss 'em back.'

Gilead did not do so. 'I suppose you have made copies in any case?'

'Wasn't necessary, I looked at them. Don't get ideas, Joe; you're washed up with the FBS, even if you brought the films and my head back on a platter. You slugged your boss – remember?'

Gilead remembered that he had not told Baldwin so. He began to believe that Baldwin did have men inside the FBS whether nis late bureau chief had been one of them or not.

'I would at least be allowed to resign with a clear record. I know Bonn – officially he would be happy to forget it. He was simply stalling for time, waiting for Baldwin to offer an opening.

'Chuck them back, Joe. I don't want to rassle. One of us might get killed – both of us, if you won the first round. You can't prove your case, because I can prove I was home teasing that cat. I sold 'copters to two *very* respectable citizens at the exact time you would claim I was somewhere else. He listened again to the speaker, answered it in the same gibberish.

Gilead's mind evaluated his own tactical situation to the same answer that Baldwin had expressed. Not being given to wishful thinking he at once tossed the films to Baldwin.

'Thanks, Joe.' He went to a small oubliette set in the wall, switched it to full power, put the films in the hopper, waited a few seconds, and switched it off. 'Good riddance to bad rubbish.'

Gilead permitted his eyebrows to climb. 'Kettle Belly, you've managed to surprise me.'

'How?'

'I thought you wanted to keep the nova effect as a means to power.'

'Nuts! Scalping a man is a hell of a poor way to cure him of dandruff. Joe, how much do you know about the nova effect?'

'Not much. I know it's a sort of atom bomb powerful enough to scare the pants off anybody who gets to thinking about it.'

'It's not a bomb. It's not a weapon. It's a means of destroying a planet and everything on it completely – by turning that planet into a nova. If that's a weapon, military or political, then I'm Samson and you're Delilah.

'But I'm not Samson,' he went on, 'and I don't propose to pull down the Temple – nor let anybody else do so. There are moral lice around who would do just that, if anybody tried to keep them from having their own way. Mrs Keithley is one such. Your boy friend Bonn is another such, if only he had the guts and the savvy – which he ain't. I'm bent on frustrating such people. What do you know about ballistics, Joe?'

'Grammar school stuff.'

'Inexcusable ignorance.' The speaker sounded again;

53

he answered it without breaking his flow. 'The problem of three bodies still lacks a neat general solution, but there are several special solutions – the asteroids that chase Jupiter in Jupiter's own orbit at the sixty degree position, for example. And there's the straight-line solution – you've heard of the asteroid "Earth-Anti"?'

'That's the chunk of rock that is always on the other side of the Sun, where we never see it.'

'That's right – only it ain't there any more. It's been novaed.'

Gilead, normally immune to surprise, had been subjected to one too many. 'Huh? I thought this nova effect was theory?'

'Nope. If you had had time to scan through the films you would have seen pictures of it. It's plutonium, lithium, and heavy water deal, with some flourishes we won't discuss. It adds up to the match that can set afire a world. It did – a little world flared up and was gone.

'Nobody saw it happen. No one on Earth could see it, for it was behind the Sun. It couldn't have been seen from Moon Colony, the Sun still blanked it off from there – visualise the geometry. All that ever saw it were a battery of cameras in a robot ship. All who knew about it were the scientists who rigged a robot ship. All who knew about it were the scientists who rigged it – and all of them were with us, except the director. If he had been, too, you would never have been in this mix up.'

'Dr. Finnley?'

'Yep. A nice guy, but a mind like a pretzel. A "political" scientist, second-rate ability. He doesn't matter; boys will ride herd on him until he's pensioned off. But we couldn't keep him from reporting and sending the film down. So I had to grab 'em and destroy them.'

'Why didn't you simply save them? All other considerations aside, they are unique in science.'

'The human race doesn't need that bit of science, not this millenium. I saved all that mattered, Joe – in my

54

head.'

'You *are* your cousin Hartley, aren't you?'

'Of course. But I'm also Kettle Belly Baldwin, and several other guys.'

'You can be Lady Godiva, for ∎ll of me.'

'As Hartley, I was entitled to those films, Joe. It was my project. I instigated it, through my boys.'

'I never credited Finnley with it. I'm not a physicist, but he obviously isn't up to it.'

'Sure, sure. I was attempting to prove that an artificial nova could not be created; the political – the racial – importance of establishing the point is obvious. It backfired on me – so we had to go into emergency action.'

'Perhaps you should have left well enough alone.'

'No. It's better to know the worst; now we can be alert for it, divert research away from it.' The speaker growled again; Baldwin went on. 'There may be a divine destiny, Joe, unlikely as it seems, that makes dangerous secrets too difficult to be broached until intelligence reaches the point where it can cope with them – if said intelligence has the will and the good intentions Ma Garver says to come up now.'

They headed for the stairs. 'I'm surprised that you leave it to an old gal like Ma to take charge during an emergency.'

'She's competent, I assure you. But I *was* running things – you heard me.'

'Oh.'

They settled down again in the above-surface study. 'I give you one more chance to back out, Joe. It doesn't matter that you know all about the films, since they are gone and you can't prove anything – but beyond that – you realise that if you come in with us, are told what is going on, you will be killed deader than a duck at the first suspicious move?'

Gilead did; he knew in fact that he was already beyond the point of no return. With the destruction of the films went his last chance of rehabilitating his former *maine persona*. This gave him no worry; the matter was done. He had become aware that from the time he had admitted that he understood the first message this man had offered him concealed in a double deck of cards he had no longer been a free actor, his moves had been constrained by moves made by Baldwin. Yet there was no help for it; his future lay here or nowhere.

'I know it; go ahead.'

'I know what your mental reservations are, Joe, you are simply accepting risk; not promising loyalty.'

'Yes – but why are you considering taking a chance on me?'

Baldwin was more serious in manner than he usually allowed himself to be. 'You're an able man, Joe. You have the savvy and the moral courage to do what is reasonable in an odd situation rather than what is conventional.'

'That's why you want me?'

'Partly that. Partly because I like the way you catch on to a new card game.' He grinned. 'And even partly because Gail likes the way you behave with a colt.'

'Gail? What's she got to do with it?'

'She reported on you to me about five minutes ago, during the raid.'

'Hmm – go ahead.'

'You've been warned.' For a moment Baldwin looked almost sheepish. 'I want you to take what I say next at its face value, Joe – don't laugh.'

'Okay.'

'You asked what I was. I'm sort of the executive secretary of this branch of an organisation of supermen.'

'I thought so.'

'Eh? How long have you known?'

'Things added up. The card game, your reaction time, I knew it when you destroyed the films.'

'Joe, what is a superman?'

Gilead did not answer.

'Very well, let's chuck the term,' Baldwin went on.

56

'It's been overused and misused and beat up until it has mostly comic connotations. I used it for shock value and I didn't shock you. The term "superman" has come to have a fairy tale meaning, conjuring up pictures of X-ray eyes, odd sense organs, double hearts, uncuttable skin, steel muscles—an adolescent's dream of the dragon-killing hero. Tripe, of course. Joe, what is a *man*? What is man that makes him more than an animal? Settle that and we'll take a crack at defining a superman – or New Man, *homo novis*, who must displace *homo sapiens* – *is* displacing him – because he is better able to survive than is *homo sap*. I'm not trying to define myself, I'll leave it up to my associates and the inexorable processes of time as to whether or not I am a superman, a member of the new species of man – same test apply to you.'

'*Me?*'

'You. You show disturbing symptoms of being *homo novis*, Joe, in a sloppy, ignorant, untrained fashion. Not likely, but you just might be one of the breed. Now – what is man? What is the one thing he can do better than animals which is so strong a survival factor that it outweighs all the things that animals of one sort or another can do much better than he can?'

'He can think.'

'I fed you that answer; no prize for it. Okay, you pass yourself off a man; let's see you do something. What is the one possible conceivable factor – or factors, if you prefer – which the hypothetical superman could have, by mutation or magic or any means, and which could be added to this advantage which man already has and which has enabled him to dominate this planet against the unceasing opposition of a million other species of fauna? Some factor that would make the domination of man by his successor as inevitable as your domination over a hound dog? Think, Joe. What is the necessary direction of evolution to the next dominant species?'

Gilead engaged in contemplation for what was for him a long time. There were so many lovely attributes that a man might have: to be able to see both like a telescope and microscope, to see the insides of things, to see throughout the spectrum, to have the hearing of the same order, to be immune to disease, to grow a new arm or leg, to fly through the air without bothering with silly gadgets like helicopters or jets, to walk unharmed the ocean bottom, to work without tiring –

Yet the eagle could fly and he was nearly extinct, even though his eyesight was better than man's. A dog has better smell and hearing, seals swim better, balance better, and furthermore can store oxygen. Rats can survive where men would starve or die of hardship; they are smart and pesky hard to kill. Rats could –

Wait! Could tougher, smarter rats displace man? No, it just wasn't in them; too small a brain.

'To be able to think better,' Gilead answered almost instantly.

'Hand the man a cigar! Superman are superthinkers; anything else is a side issue. I'll allow the possibility of super-somethings which might exterminate or dominate mankind other than by outsmarting him in his own racket – thought. But I deny that it is possible for a *man* to conceive in discreet terms what such a super-something would be or how this something would win out. New Man will beat out *homo sap* in *homo sap's* own speciality – rational thought, the ability to recognise data, store them, integrate them, evaluate correctly the result, and arrive at a correct decision. That is how man got to be champion; the creature who can do it better is the coming champion. Sure, there are other survival factors, good health, good sense organs, fast reflexes, but they aren't even comparable, as the long, rough history of mankind has proved over and over – Marat in his bath, Roosevelt in his wheelchair, Caesar with his epilepsy and his bad stomach, Nelson with one eye and one arm, blind Milton; when the chips are down it's *brain* that wins, not the body's tools.'

'Stop a moment,' said Gilead. 'How about E.S.P.?'

Baldwin shrugged. 'I'm not sneering at extra-sensory perception any more than I would at exceptional eyesight – E.S.P. is not in the same league with ability to think correctly. E.S.P. is a grab bag name for the means other than the known sense organs by which the brain may gather data – but the trick that pays off with first prize is to make use of that data, to *reason* about it. If you would like a telepathic hook up to Shanghai, I can arrange it; we've got operators at both ends – but you can get whatever data you might happen to need from Shanghai by phone with less trouble, less chance of a bad connection, and less danger of somebody listening in. Telepaths can't pick up a radio message, it's not the same waveband.'

'What waveband is it?'

'Later, later, You've got a lot to learn.'

'I wasn't thinking especially of telepathy. I was thinking of all parapsychological phenomena.'

'Same reasoning. Apportation would be nice, if telekinetics had gotten that far – which it ain't. But a pick-up truck moves things handily enough. Television in the hands of an intelligent man counts for more than clairvoyance in a moron. Quit wasting my time, Joe.'

'Sorry.'

'We defined thinking as integrating data and arriving at correct answers. Look around you. Most people do that stunt just well enough to get to the corner store and back without breaking a leg. If the average man thinks at all, he does silly things like generalising from a single datum. He uses one-valued logics. If he is exceptionally bright, he may use two-valued, "either-or" logic to arrive at his wrong answers. If he is hungry, hurt, or personally interested in the answer, he can't use any sort of logic and will discard an observed fact as blithely as he will stake his life on a piece of wishful thinking. He uses the technical miracles created by superior men without wonder or surprise, as a kitten accepts a bowl of milk. Far from aspiring to higher reasoning, he is not even aware that higher reasoning exists. He classes his own mental process as being of the same sort as the genius of an Einstein. Man is not a rational animal; he is a rationalising animal.

'For explanations of a universe that confuses him he seizes on to numerology, astrology, hysterical religions, and other fancy ways to go crazy. Having accepted such glorified nonsense, facts make no impression on him, even if at the cost of his own life. Joe, one of the hardest things to believe is the abysmal depth of human stupidity.

'That is why there is always room at the top, why a man with just a *leetle* more on the ball can so easily become governor, millionaire, or college president – and why *homo sap* is sure to be displaced by New Man, because there is so much room for improvement and evolution never stops.

'Here and there among ordinary men is a rare individual who really thinks, can and does use logic in at least one field – he's often as stupid as the rest outside his study or laboratory – but he can think, if he's not disturbed or sick or frightened. This rare individual is responsible for *all* the progress made by the race; the others reluctantly adopt his results. Much as the ordinary man dislikes and distrusts and persecutes the process of thinking he is forced to accept the results occasionally, because thinking is efficient compared with his own maunderings. He may still plant his corn in the dark of the Moon but he will plant better corn developed by better men than he.

'Still rarer is the man who thinks habitually, who applies reason, rather than habit pattern, to all his activity. Unless he masques himself, his is a dangerous life; he is regarded as queer, untrustworthy, subversive of public morals; he is a pink monkey among brown monkeys – a fatal mistake. Unless the pink monkey can dye himself brown before he is caught.

'The brown monkey's instinct to kill is correct; such men are dangerous to all monkey customs.

'Rarest of all is the man who can and does reason

at all times, quickly, accurately, inclusively, despite hope
or fear or bodily distress, without egocentric bias or
thalmic disturbance, with correct memory, with clear
distinction between fact, assumption and non-fact. Such
men exist, Joe; they are "New Man" – human in all
respects, indistinguishable in appearance or under the
scalpel from *homo sap,* yet as unlike him in action as
the Sun is unlike a single candle.'

Gilead said, 'Are you that sort?

'You will continue to form your own opinions.'

'And you think I may be, too?'

'Could be. I'll have more data in a few days.'

Gilead laughed until the tears came. 'Kettle Belly, if
I'm the future hope of the race, they had better send in
the second team quick. Sure I'm brighter than most of
the jerks I run into, but, as you say, the competition
isn't stiff. But I haven't any sublime aspirations. I've got
as lecherous an eye as the next man. I enjoy wasting
time over a glass of beer, I just don't *feel* like a superman.'

'Speaking of beer, let's have some.' Baldwin got up and
obtained two cans of the brew. 'Remember that Mowgli
felt like a wolf. Being a New Man does not divorce you
from human sympathies and pleasures. There have been
New Men all through history. I doubt if most of them suspected that their difference entitled them to call themselves a different breed. Then they went ahead and bred
with the daughters of men, diffusing their talents through
the racial organism, preventing them from effectuating
until chance brought the genetic factors together again.'

'Then I take it that New Man is not a special mutation?'

'Huh? Who isn't a mutation, Joe? All of us are a
collection of millions of mutations. Around the globe
hundreds of mutations have taken place in our human
germ plasm while we have been sitting here. No, *homo
novis* didn't come about because great grandfather stood
too close to a cyclotron; *homo novis* was not even a

separate breed until he became aware of himself, organised, and decided to hang on to what his genes had handed him. You could mix New Man back into the race today and lose him; he's merely a variation becoming a species. A million years from now is another matter; I venture to predict that New Man, of that year and model, won't be able to interbreed with *homo sap* – no viable offspring.'

'You don't expect present man – *homo sapiens* – to disappear?'

'Not necessarily. The dog adapted to man. Probably more dogs now than in umpteen B.C. – and better fed.'

'And man would be New Man's dog.'

'Again not necessarily. Consider the cat.'

'The idea is to skim the cream of the race's germ plasm and keep it biologically separate until the two races are permanently distinct. You chaps sound like a bunch of stinkers, Kettle Belly.'

'Monkey talk.'

'Perhaps. The new race would necessarily run things –'

'Do you expect New Man to decide grave matters by counting common man's runny noses?'

'No, that was my point. Postulating such a new race, the result is inevitable. Kettle Belly, I confess to a monkey prejudice in favour of democracy, human dignity, and freedom. It goes beyond logic; it is the kind of a world I like. In my job I have jungled with the outcasts of society, shared their slum-gullion. Stupid they may be, bad they are not – I have no wish to see them become domestic animals.'

For the first time the big man showed concern. His *persona* as 'King of the Kopters,' master merchandiser, slipped away; he sat in brooding majesty, a lonely and unhappy figure. 'I know, Joe. They are of us; their little dignities, their nobilities, are not lessened by their sorry state. Yet it must be.'

'Why? New Man will come – granted, But why hurry the process?'

'Ask yourself.' He swept a hand toward the oubliette.

'Ten minutes ago you and I saved this planet, all our race. It's the hour of the knife. Some one must be on guard if the race is to live; there is no one but us. To guard effectively we new men must be organised, must never fumble any crises like this – and must increase our numbers. We are few now, Joe, as the crises increase, we must increase to meet them. Eventually – and it's a dead race with time – we must take over and make certain that baby never plays with matches.'

He stopped and brooded. 'I confess to that same affection for democracy, Joe. But it's like yearning for the Santa Claus you believed in as a child. For a hundred and fifty years or so democracy, or something like it, could flourish safely. The issues were such as to be settled without disaster by the votes of common men, befogged and ignorant as they were. But now, if the race is simply to stay alive, political decisions depend on real knowledge of such things as nuclear physics, planetary ecology, genetic theory, even system mechanics. They aren't up to it, Joe. With goodness and more will than they possess less than one in a thousand could stay awake over one page of nuclear physics; they can't learn what they must know.'

Gilead brushed it aside. 'It's up to us to brief them. Their hearts are all right; tell them the score – they'll come down with the right answers.'

'No, Joe. We've tried it; it does not work. As you say, most of them are good, the way a dog can be noble and good. Yet there are bad ones – Mrs Keithley and company and more like her. Reason is poor propaganda when opposed by the yammering, unceasing lies of shrewd and evil and self-serving men. The little man has no way to judge and the shoddy lies are packaged more attractively. There is no way to offer colour to a colourblind man, nor is there any way for us to give the man of imperfect brain the canny skill to distinguish a lie from a truth.

'No, Joe. The gulf between us and them is narrow, but

63

it is very deep. We cannot close it.'

'I wish,' said Gilead, 'that you wouldn't class me with your "New Man"; I feel more at home on the other side.'

'You will decide for yourself which side you are on, as each of us has done.'

Gilead forced a change in subject. Ordinarily immune to thalamic disturbance this issue upset him; his brain followed Baldwin's argument and assured him that it was true; his inclinations fought it. He was confronted with the sharpest of all tragedy; two equally noble and valid rights, utterly opposed. 'What do you people do, aside from stealing films?'

'Mmm – many things.' Baldwin relaxed, looked again like a jovial sharp businessman. 'Where a push here and a touch there will keep things from going to pot, we apply the pressure, by many and devious means. And we scout for suitable material and bring it into the fold when we can – we've had our eye on you for ten years.'

'So.'

'Yep. That is a prime enterprise. Through public data we eliminate all but about one tenth of one per cent; that thousandth individual we watch. And then there are our horticultural societies.' He grinned.

'Finish your joke.'

'We weed people.'

'Sorry, I'm slow today.'

'Joe, didn't you ever feel a yen to wipe out some evil, obscene, rotten jerk who infected everything he touched, yet was immune to legal action? We treat them as cancers; we excise them from the body social. We keep a "Better Dead" list; when a man is clearly morally bankrupt we close his account at the first opportunity.'

Gilead smiled. 'If you were sure what you are doing, it could be fun.'

'We are always sure, though our methods would be no good in a monkey law court. Take Mrs Keithley – is there doubt in your mind?'

'None.'

'Why don't you have her indicted? Don't bother to answer. For example, two weeks from tonight there will be giant pow-wow of the new, rejuvenated, bigger-and-better-than-ever Ku Klux Klan on a mountain top down Carolina way. When the fun is at its height, when they are mouthing obscenities, working each other up to the pogram spirit ,an act of God is going to wipe out the whole kit and kaboodle. Very sad.'

'Could I get in on that?'

'You aren't even a cadet as yet.' Baldwin went on, There is the project to increase our numbers, but that is a thousand-year programme; you'd need a perpetual calendar to check it. More important is keeping matches away from baby. Joe, it's been eighty-five years since we beheaded the last commissar: have you wondered why so little basic progress in science has been made in that time?'

'Eh? There have been a lot of changes.'

'Minor adaptation – some spectacular, almost none of them basic. Of course there was very little progress made under communism; a totalitarian political religion is incompatible with free investigation. Let me digress: the communist inter-regnum was responsible for the New Men getting together and organising. Most New Men are scientists, for obvious reasons. When the commissars started ruling on natural laws by political criteria – Lysenko-ism and similar nonsense – it did not sit well; a lot of us went underground.

'I'll skip the details. It brought us together, gave us practice in underground activity, and gave a backlog of new research, carried out underground. Some of it was obviously dangerous; we decided to hang on to it for a while. Since then such secret knowledge has grown, for we never give out an item until it has been scrutinised for social hazards. Since much of it is dangerous and since very few indeed outside our organisation are capable of real original thinking, basic science has been almost at a – public! – standstill.

'We hadn't expected to have to do it that way. We

helped to see to it that the new constitution was liberal and – we thought – workable. But the new Republic turned out to be an even poorer thing than the old. The evil ethic of communism had corrupted, even after the form was gone. We held off. Now we know that we must hold off until we can revise the whole society.'

'Kettle Belly,' Joe said slowly, 'you speak as if you had been on the spot. How old are you?'

'I'll tell you when you are the age I am now. A man has lived long enough when he no longer longs to live. I ain't there yet. Joe, I must have your answer, or this must be continued in our next.'

'You had it at the beginning – but, see here, Kettle Belly, there is one job I want promised to me.'

'Which is?'

'I want to kill Mrs Keithley.'

'Keep your pants on. When you're trained, and if she's still alive then you'll be used for that purpose –'

'Thanks.'

'– provided you are the proper tool for it.' Baldwin turned towards the mike, called out, 'Gail' and added one word in the strange tongue.

Gail showed up promptly. 'Joe,' said Baldwin, 'when this young lady gets through with you, you will be able to sing, whistle, chew gum, play chess, hold your breath, and fly a kite simultaneously – and all this while riding a bicycle under water. Take him, sis, he's all yours.'

Gail rubbed her hands. 'Oh, boy!'

'First we must teach you to see and to hear, then to remember, then to speak, and then to think.'

Joe looked at her. 'What's this I'm doing with my mouth at this moment?'

'It's not talking, it's a sort of grunting. And English is not structurally suited to thinking. Shut up and listen.'

In their underground classroom Gail had available several types of apparatus to record and manipulate light and sound. She commenced throwing groups of figures on a screen, in flashes. 'What was it, Joe?'

'Nine-six-oh-seven-two – That was as far as I got.'

'It was up there a full thousandth of a second. Why did you get only the left hand side of the group?'

'That's as far as I had read.'

'Look at all of it. Don't make an effort of will; just look at it.' She flashed another number.

Joe's memory was naturally good; his intelligence was high – just how high he did not yet know. Unconvinced that the drill was useful, he relaxed and played along. Soon he was beginning to grasp a nine-digit array as a single *gestalt;* Gail reduced the flash time.

'What is this magic lantern gimmick?' he inquired.

'It's a Renshaw tachistoscope. Back to work.'

Around World War II Dr Samuel Renshaw at the Ohio State University was proving that most people are about one-fifth efficient in using their capacities to see, hear, taste, feel, and remember. His research was swallowed in the morass of communist pseudoscience that obtained after World War III, but, after his death, his findings were preserved underground. Gail did not expose Gilead to the odd language he had heard until he had been rather thoroughly Renshawed.

However, from the time of his interview with Baldwin the other persons at the ranch used it in his presence. Sometimes someone – usually Ma Garver – would translate, sometimes not. He was flattered to feel accepted, but gravelled to know that it was at the lowest cadetship. He was a child among adults.

Gail started teaching him to hear by speaking to him single words from the odd language, requiring him to repeat them back. 'No, Joe. Watch.' This time when she spoke the word it appeared on the screen in sound analysis, by a means basically like one long used to show the deaf-and-dumb their speech mistakes. 'Now you try it.'

He did, the two arrays hung side by side. 'How's that, teacher?' he said triumphantly.

'Terrible, by several decimal places. You held the final

guttural too long – ' She pointed. 'The middle vowel was formed with your tongue too high and you pitched it too low and you failed to let the pitch rise. And six other things. You couldn't possibly have been understood. I heard what you said, but it was gibberish. Try again. And don't call me "teacher".'

'Yes, ma'am,' he answered solemnly.

She shifted the controls; he tried again. This time his analysis array was laid down on top of hers; where the two matched, they cancelled. Where they did not match, his errors stood out in contrasting colours. The screen looked like a sun burst.

'Try again, Joe.' She repeated the work without letting it affect the display.

'Confound it, if you would tell me what the words mean instead of treating me the way Milton treated his daughters about Latin, I could remember them easier.'

She shrugged. 'I can't, Joe. You must learn to hear and to speak first. Speedtaik is a flexible language; the same word it not likely to recur. This practice word means: "The far horizons draw no nearer." That's not much help, is it?'

The definition seemed improbable, but he was learning not to doubt her. He was not used to women who were always two jumps ahead of him. He ordinarily felt sorry for the poor little helpless cuddly creatures; this one he often wanted to slug. He wondered if this response were what the romancers meant by 'love'; he decided that it couldn't be.

'Try again, Joe.' Speedtalk was a structurally different speech from any the race had ever used. Long before, Ogden and Richards had shown that eight hundred and fifty words were sufficient vocabulary to express anything that could be expressed by 'normal' human vocabularies, with the aid of a handful of special words – a hundred odd – for each special field, such as horse racing or ballistics. About the same time phoneticians has analysed all human tongues into about a hundred-odd sounds, represented by the letters of a general phonetic alphabet. On these two propositions Speedtalk was based.

To be sure, the phonetic alphabet was much less in number than the words in Basic English. But the letters representing sounds in the phonetic alphabet were each capable of variation several different ways – length, stress, pitch, rising, falling. The more trained an ear was the larger the number of possible variations but, without much refinement of accepted phonetic practice, it was possible to establish a one-to-one relationship with basic English so the *one phonetic symbol* was equivalent to an entire word in a 'normal' language, one Speedtalk word was equal to an entire sentence. The language consequently was learned by letter units rather than by word units – but each word was spoken and listened to as a single structural gestalt.

But Speedtalk was not 'shorthand' Basic English. 'Normal' languages, having their root in days of superstition and ignorance, have in them inherently and unescapably wrong structures of mistaken ideas about the universe. One can think logically in English only by extreme effort, so bad it is as a mental tool. For example, the verb 'to be' in English has twenty-one distinct meanings, *every single one of which is false-to-fact*.

A symbolic structure, invented instead of accepting without question, can be made similar in structure to the real-world to which it refers. The structure of Speedtalk did *not* contain the hidden errors of English; it was structured as much like the real world as the New Men could make it. For example, it did not contain the unreal distinction between nouns and verbs found in most other languages. The world – the continuum known to science and including all human activity – does not contain 'noun things' and 'verb things'; it contains space-time events and relationships between them. The advantage for achieving truth, or something more nearly like truth, was similar to the advantage of keeping account books in Arabic numerals rather than Roman.

All other languages made scientific, multi-valued logic almost impossible to achieve; in Speedtalk it was as difficult *not* to be logical. Compare the pellucid Boolean logic with the obscurities of the Aristotelean logic it supplanted.

Paradoxes are verbal, do not exist in the real world – and Speedtalk did not have such built into it. Who shaves the Spanish Barber? Answer: follow him around and see. In the syntax of Speedtalk the paradox of the Spanish Barber could not even be expressed, save as a self-evident error.

But Joe Greene-Gilead-Briggs could not learn it until he had learned to hear, by learning to speak. He slaved away; the screen continued to remain lighted with his errors.

Came finally a time when Joe's pronunciation of a sentence-word blanked out Gail's sample; the screen turned dark. He felt more triumph over that than anything he could remember.

His delight was short. By a circuit Gail had thoughtfully added some days earlier the machine answered with a flourish of trumpets, loud applause, and then added in a cooing voice, 'Mama's *good* boy!'

He turned to her. 'Woman, you spoke of matrimony. If you ever do manage to marry me, I'll beat you.'

'I haven't made up my mind about you yet,' she answered evenly. 'Now try this word, Joe –'

Baldwin showed up that evening, called him aside. 'Joe! C'mere. Listen, lover boy, you keep your animal nature out of your work, or I'll have to find you a new teacher.'

'But –'

'You heard me. Take her swimming, take her riding, after hours you are on your own. Work time – strictly business. I've got plans for you; I want you to get smarted up.'

'She complained about me?'

70

'Don't be silly. It's my business to know what's going on.'

'Hmmm. Kettle Belly, what is this shopping-for-a-husband she kids about? Is she serious, or is it just intended to rattle me?'

'Ask her. Not that it matters, as you won't have any choice if she means it. She has the calm persistence of the law of gravitation.'

'Ouch! I had had the impression that the "New Man' did not bother with marriage and such like, as you put it, "monkey customs".'

'Some do, some don't. Me, I've been married quite a piece, but I mind a mousy little member of our lodge who has had nine kids by nine fathers – all wonderful genius-plus kids. On the other hand I can point out one with eleven kids – Thalia Wagner – who has never so much as looked at another man. Geniuses make their own rules in such matters, Joe; they always have. Here are some established statistical facts about genius, as shown by Armatoe's work –'

He ticked them off. 'Geniuses are usually long lived. they are not modest, not honestly so. They have infinite capacity for taking pains. They are emotionally indifferent to accepted codes of morals – they make their own rules. You seem to have the stigmata, by the way.'

'Thanks for nothing. Maybe I should have a new teacher, if there is anyone else available who can do it.'

'*Any of us can do it, just as anybody handy teaches* a baby to talk. She's actually a biochemist, when she has time for it.'

'When she has time?'

'Be careful of that kid, son. Her real profession is the same as yours – honourable hatchet man. She's killed upwards of three hundred people.' Kettle Belly grinned. 'If you want to switch teachers, just drop me a wink.'

Gilead-Greene hastily changed the subject. 'You were speaking of work for me: How about Mrs Keithley? Is she still alive?'

71

'Yes, blast her.'

'Remember, I've got dibs on her.'

'You may have to go to the Moon to get her. She's reported to be building a vacation home there. Old age seems to be telling on her; you had better get on with your homework if you want a crack at her.' Moon Colony even then was a centre of geriatrics for the rich. The low gravity was easy on their hearts, made them feel young – and possibly extended their lives.

'Okay, I will.'

Instead of asking for a new teacher Joe took a highly polished apple to their next session. Gail ate it, leaving him very little core, and put him harder to work than ever. While perfecting his hearing and pronunciation, she started him on the basic thousand-letter vocabulary by forcing him to start to talk simple three and four letter sentences, and by answering him in different word-sentences using the same phonetic letters. Some of the vowel and consonant sequences were very difficult to pronounce.

Master them he did. He had been used to doing most things easier than could those around him; now he was in very fast company. He stretched himself and began to achieve part of his own large latent capacity. When he began to catch some of the dinner-table conversation and to reply in simple Speedtalk – being forbidden by Gail to answer in English – she started him on the ancillary vocabularies.

An economical language cannot be limited to a thousand words; although almost every idea can be expressed somehow in a short vocabulary, higher orders of abstracttion are convenient. For technical words Speedtalk employed an open expansion of sixty of the thousand-odd phonetic letters. They were the letters ordinarily used as numerals; by preceding a number with a letter used for no other purpose, the symbol was designated as having a word value.

New Men numbered to the base sixty – three times four

times five, a convenient, easily factored system, most economical, i.e., the symbol '100' identified the number described in English as thirty-six hundred – yet permitting quick in-the-head translation from common notation to Speedtalk fugures and *vice versa*.

By using these figures, each prefaced by the indicator – a voiceless Welsh or Burmese '1' – a pool of 215,999 words (one less than the cube of sixty) were available for specialised meaning without using more than four letters including the indicator. Most of them could be pronounced as one syllable. These had not the stark simplicity of basic Speedtalk; nevertheless words such as 'ischthyophagous' and 'constitutionality' were thus compressed to monosyllables. Such short cuts can best be appreciated by anyone who has heard a long speech in Cantonese translated into a short speech in English. Yet English is not the most terse of 'normal' languages – and expanded Speedtalk is many times more economical than the briefest of 'normal' tongues.

By adding one more letter (sixty to the fourth power) just short of thirteen *million* words could be added if needed – and most of them could still be pronounced as one syllable.

When Joe discovered that Gail expected him to learn a couple of hundred thousand new words in a matter of days, he baulked. 'Damn it, Fancy Pants, I am not a superman. I'm here by mistake.'

'Your opinion is worthless; I think you can do it. Now listen.'

'Suppose I flunk; does that put me safely off your list of possible victims?"

'If you flunk, I wouldn't have you on toast. Instead I'd tear your head off and stuff it down your throat. But you won't flunk; I *know*. However,' she added, 'I'm not sure you would be a satisfactory husband; you argue too much.'

He made a brief and bitter remark in Speedtalk; she answered with one word which described his shortcomings in detail. They got to work.

Joe was mistaken; he learned the expanded vocabulary as fast as he heard it. He had a latent eidetic memory; the Renshawing process now enabled him to use it fully. And his mental processes, always fast, had become faster than he knew.

The ability to learn Speedtalk at all is proof of supernormal intelligence; the *use* of it by such intelligence renders that mind efficient. Even before World War II Alfred Korzybski had shown that human thought was performed, when done efficiently, only in symbols; the action of 'pure' thought, free of abstracted speech symbols, was merely fantasy. The brain was so constructed as to work without symbols only on the animal level; to speak of 'reasoning' without symbols was to speak nonsense.

Speedtalk did not merely speed up communication – by its structures it made thought more logical; by its economy it made thought processes enormously faster, since it takes almost as long to *think* a word as it does to speak it.

Korzybski's monumental work went fallow during the communist interregnum; *Das Kapital* is a childish piece of work, when analysed by semantics, so the politburo suppressed semantics – and replaced it by *ersatz* under the same name, as Lysenkoism replaced the science of genetics.

Having Speedtalk to help him learn *more* Speedtalk, Joe learned very rapidly. The Renshawing had continued; he was now able to grasp a *gestalt* or configuration in many senses at once, grasp it, remember it, reason about it with great speed.

Living time is not calendar time, a man's life is the thought that flows through his brain. Any man capable of learning Speedtalk had an association time at least three times as fast as an ordinary man. Speedtalk itself enabled him to manipulate symbols approximately seven times as fast as English symbols could be manipulated.

Seven times three is twenty-one; a new man had an *effective* life times of at least *sixteen hundred years*, reckoned in flow of ideas.

They had time to become encyclopaedic synthesists, something denied any ordinary man by the strait-jacket of his sort of time.

When Joe had learned to talk, to read and write and cipher, Gail turned him over to others for his real education. But before she checked him out she played him several dirty tricks.

For three days she forbade him to eat. When it was evident that he could think and keep his temper despite low blood-sugar count, despite hunger reflex, she added sleeplessness and pain – intense, long continued, and varied pain. She tried subtly to goad him into irrational action; he remained bedrock steady, his mind clicking away at any assigned task as dependably as an electronic computer.

'Who's not a superman?' she asked at the end of their last session.

'Yes, teacher.'

'Come here, lug.' She grabbed him by the ears, kissed him soundly. 'So long.' He did not see her again for many weeks.

His tutor in E.S.P. was an ineffectual little man who had taken the protective colouration of the name Weems. Joe was not very good at producing E.S.P. phenomena. Clairvoyance he did not appear to have. He was better at precognition, but he did not improve with practice. He was best at telekinesis; he could have made a soft living with dice. But, as Kettle Belly had pointed out, from affecting the roll of dice to moving tons of freight was quite a gap – and one possibly not worth bridging.

'It may have other uses, however,' Weems had said softly, lapsing into English. 'Consider what might be done if one could influence the probability that a neutron would reach a particular nucleus – or change the statistical probability in a mass.'

75

Gilead let it ride, it was an outrageous thought.

At telepathy he was erratic to exasperation. He called the Rhine cards once without a miss, then had poor scores for three weeks. More highly structured communication seemed quite beyond him, until one day without apparent cause but during an attempt to call the cards by telepathy, he found himself hooked in with Weems for all of ten seconds – time enough for a thousand words by Speedtalk standards.

– It comes out as speech!

– Why not? Thought is speech.

– How do we do it?

– If we knew it would not be so unreliable. As it is, some can do it by volition, some by accident, and some never seem to be able to do it. We do know this: while thought may not be of the physical world in any fashion we can now define and manipulate, it is similar to events in continuum in its quantal nature. You are now studying the extension of the quantuum concept to all features of the continuum, you know the chronon, the mensum, and the viton, as quanta, as well as the action units of quanta such as photon. The continuum has not only structure but texture in all its features. The least unit of thought we term the psychon.

– Define it, put salt on its tail.

– Some day, some day. I can tell you this; the fastest possible rate of thought is one psychon per chronon; this is a basic, universal constant.

– How close do we come to that?

– Less than sixty-to-the-minus-third-power of the possibility.

– Better creatures than ourselves will follow us. We pick pebbles at a boundless ocean.

– What can we do to improve it?

– Gather our pebbles with serene minds.

Gilead paused for a long split second of thought. *– Can psychons be destroyed?*

– Vitons may be transferred, psychons are –

76

The connection was suddenly destroyed. 'As I was saying.' Weems went on quietly, 'psychons are as yet beyond our comprehension in many respects. Theory indicates that they may not be destroyed, that thought, like action, is persistent. Whether or not such theory, if true, means that personal identity is also persistent must remain an open question. See the daily papers – a few hundred years from now – or a few hundred thousand. He stood up.

'I'm anxious to try tomorrow's session, Doc,' Gilead-Grene almost bubbled. 'Maybe –'

'I'm finished with you.'

'But, Doctor Weems, that connection was clear as a phone hook up. Perhaps tomorrow –'

'We have established that your talent is erratic. We have no way to train it to dependability. Time is too short to waste, mine and yours.' Lapsing suddenly into English, he added, 'No.'

Gilead left.

During his training in other fields Joe was exposed to many things best described as impressive gadgets. There was an integrating pantograph, a factory-in-a-box, which the New Men planned to turn over to ordinary men as soon as the social system was no longer dominated by economic wolves. It could and did reproduce almost any prototype placed on its stage, requiring thereto only materials and power. Its power came from a little nucle-onics motor the size of Joe's thumb; its theory played hob with conventional notions of entropy. One put in 'sausage,' one got out 'pig.'

Latent in it was the shape of an economic system as different from the current one as the assembly-line economy differed from the family-shop system – and in such a system lay possibilities of human freedom and dignity missing for centuries, if they had ever existed.

In the meantime New Men rarely bought more than one of anything – a pattern. Or they made a pattern.

77

Another useful but hardly wonderful gadget was a dictaphone-typewriter-printing-press combination. The machine's analysers recognised each of the thousand-odd phonetic symbols; there was a typebar for each sound. It produced one or many copies. Much of Gilead's education came from pages printed by this gadget, saving the precious time of others.

The arrangement, classification, and accessibility of knowledge remains in all ages the most pressing problem. With the New Men, complete and organised memory licked most of the problem and rendered record keeping, most reading and writing – and most especially the time-destroying trouble of re-reading – unnecessary. The auto-scriber gadget, combined with a 'librarian' machine that could 'hear' that portion of Speedtalk built into it as a filing system, covered most of the rest of the problem. New Men were not cluttered with endless bits of paper. They *never* wrote memoranda.

The area under the ranch was crowded with techno-logical wonders, all newer than next week. Incredibly tiny manipulators for micrurgy of all sorts, surgical, chemical, biological manipulation oddities of cybernetics only less complex than the human brain – the list is too long to describe. Joe did not study all of them; an encyclo-paedic synthesist is concerned with structured shapes of knowledge; he cannot, even with Speedtalk, study details in every field.

Early in his education, when it was clear that he had had the potential to finish the course, plastic surgery was started to give him a new identity and basic appearance. His height was reduced by three inches; his skull was somewhat changed; his complexion was permanently darkened. Gail picked the facial appearance he was given; he did not object. He rather liked it; seemed to fit his new inner personality.

With a new face, a new brain, and a new outlook, he was almost in fact a new man. Before he had been a natural genius; now he was a *trained* genius.

'Joe, how about some riding?'

'Suits.'

'I want to give War Conqueror some gentle exercise. He's responding to the saddle; I don't want him to forget.'

'Right with you.'

Kettle Belly and Gilead-Greene rode out from the ranch buildings. Baldwin let the young horse settle to a walk and began to talk. 'I figure you are about ready for work, son.' Even in Speedtalk Kettle Belly's speech retained his own flavour.

'I suppose so, but I still have those mental reservations.'

'Not sure we are on the side of the angels?'

'I'm sure you mean to be. It's evident that the organisation selects for good will and humane intentions quite as carefully as for ability. I wasn't sure at one time –'

'Yes?'

'That candidate who came here about six months ago, the one who broke his neck in a riding accident.'

'Oh, yes! Very sad.'

'Very opportune, you mean, Kettle Belly.'

'Damn it, Joe, if a bad apple gets in this far, we can't let him out.' Baldwin reverted to English for swearing purposes; he maintained that it had 'more juice.'

'I know it. That's why I'm sure about the quality of our people.'

'So its "our people" now?'

'Yes. But I'm not sure we are on the right track.'

'What's your notion of the right track?'

'We should come out of hiding and teach the ordinary man what he can learn of what we know. He could learn a lot of it and could use it. Properly briefed and trained, he could run his affairs pretty well. He would gladly kick out the no-goods who ride on his shoulders, if only he knew how. We could show him. That would be more to the point than this business of spot assassination, now

79

and then, here and there – mind you, I don't object to killing any man who merits killing; I simply say it's inefficient. No doubt we would have to continue to guard against such crises as the one that brought you and me together, but, in the main, people could run their own affairs if we would just stop pretending that we are so scared we can't mix with people, come out of our hole, and lend a hand.'

Baldwin reined up. 'Don't say that I don't mix with the common people, Joe; I sell used 'copters for a living. You can't get any commoner. And don't imply that my heart is not with them. We are not like them, but we are tied to them by the strongest bond of all, for we are all, each every one, sickening with the same certainly fatal desease – we are alive.

'As for our killings, you don't understand the principles of assassination as a political weapon. Read –' He named a Speedtalk library designation. 'If I were knocked off, our organisation wouldn't even hiccup, but organisations for bad purposes are different. They are personal empires; if you pick the time and the method, you can destroy such an organisation by killing one man – the parts that remain will be almost harmless until assimilated by another leader – then you kill *him*. It is not inefficient; it's quite efficient, if planned with the brain and not with the emotions.

'As for keeping ourselves separate, we are about like the U-235 in U-238, not effective unless separated out. There have been potential New Men in every generation, but they were spread too thin.

As for keeping our existence secret, it is utterly necessary if we are to survive and increase. There is nothing so dangerous as being the Chosen People – and in the minority. One group was persecuted for two thousand years merely for making the claim.'

He again shifted to English to swear. 'Damn it, Joe, face up to it. This world is run the way my great aunt Susie flies a 'copter. Speedtalk or no Speedtalk, common

80

man *can't* learn to cope with modern problems. No use to talk about the unused potential of his brain, he has not got the *will* to learn what he would have to know. We can't fit him out with new genes, so we have to lead him by the hand to keep him from killing himself – and us. We can give him personal liberty, we can give him autonomy in most things, we can give him a great measure of personal dignity – and we will, because we believe that individual freedom, at all levels, is the direction of evolution, of maximum survival value. But we can't let him fiddle with issues of racial life and death; he ain't up to it.

'No help for it. Each shape of society develops its own ethic. We are shaping this the way we are inexorably forced to, by the logic of events. We *think* we are shaping it towards survival.'

'Are we?' mused Greene-Gilead.

'Remains to be seen. Survivors survive. We'll know – Wup! Meeting's adjourned.'

The radio on Baldwin's pommel was shrilling his personal emergency call. He listened, then spoke one sharp word in Speedtalk. 'Back to the house, Joe!' He wheeled and was away. Joe's mount came of less selected stock; he was forced to follow.

Baldwin sent for Joe soon after he got back. Joe went in; Gail was already there.

Baldwin's face was without expression. He said in English, 'I've work for you, Joe, work you won't have any doubt about. Mrs Keithley.'

'Good.'

'Not good.' Baldwin shifted to Speedtalk. 'We have been caught flat-footed. Either the second set of films was never destroyed, or there was a third set. We do not know; the man who could tell us is dead. But Mrs Keithley obtained a set and has been using them.

'This is the situation. The "fuse" of the Nova effect has been installed in the New Age Hotel. It has been sealed off and can be triggered only by radio signal from the Moon – her signal. The "fuse" has been rigged so that any attempt to break in, as long as the firing circuit is still armed, will trigger it and set it off. Even an attempt to examine it by penetration wavelengths will set it off. Speaking as a physicist, it is my considered opinion that *no* plan for tackling the "Nova" fuse bomb itself will work unless the arming circuit is first broken on the Moon and that no attempt should be made to get at fuse before then, because of extreme danger to the entire planet.

'The arming circuit and the radio relay to the Earth-side trigger is located on the Moon in a building inside her private dome. The triggering control she keeps with her. From the same control she can disarm the arming circuit temporarily; it is a combination dead-man switch and time-clock arrangement. It can be set to disarm for a maximum of twelve hours, to let her sleep, or possibly to permit her to order rearrangements. Unless it is switched off any attempt to enter the building in which the arming circuit is housed will also trigger the "Nova" bomb circuit. While it is disarmed, the housing on the Moon may be broached by force but this will set off alarms which will warn her to rearm and then to trigger at once. The set up is such that the following sequence of events must take place:

'First, she must be killed, and the circuit disarmed.

'Second, the building housing the arming circuit and radio relay to the trigger must be broken open and the circuits destroyed *before* the time clock can rearm and trigger. This must be done with speed, not only because of guards, but because her surviving lieutenants will attempt to seize power by possessing themselves of the controls.

'Third, as soon as word is received on Earth that the arming circuit is destroyed, the New Age will be attacked in force and the "Nova" bomb destroyed.

'Fourth, as soon as the bomb is destroyed, a general round up must be made of all persons technically capable of setting up the "Nova" effect from plans. This alert must be maintained until it is certain that no plans remain in existence, including the third set of films, and further established by hypno that no competent person possesses sufficient knowledge to set it up without plans. This alert may compromise our secret status; the risk must be taken.

'Any questions?'

'Kettle Belly,' said Joe, 'doesn't she know that if the Earth become a Nova, the Moon will be swallowed up in the disaster?'

'Crater walls shield her dome from line-of-sight with Earth; apparently she believes she is safe. Evil is essentially stupid, Joe; despite her brilliance, she believes what she wishes to believe. Or it may by that she is willing to risk her own death against the tempting prize of absolute power. Her plan is to proclaim power with some pious nonsense about being high priestess of peace – a euphemism for Empress of Earth. It is a typical paranoid deviation; the proof of the craziness lies in the fact that the physical arrangements make it certain – if we do not intervene – that Earth will be destroyed automatically a few hours after her death; a thing that could happen any time – and a compelling reason for all speed. No one has ever quite managed to conquer all of Earth, not even the commissars. Apparently she wishes not only to conquer it, but wants to destroy it after she is gone, lest anyone else ever manage to do so again. Any more questions?'

He went on, 'The plan is this:

'You two will go to the Moon to become domestic servants to Mr. and Mrs Alexander Copley, a rich, elderly couple living at the Elysian Rest Homes, Moon Colony. They are of us. Shortly they will decide to return to Earth; you two will decide to remain, you like it. You will advertise, offering to work for anyone who will post your return bond. About this time Mrs Keithley will have lost through circumstances that will be arranged, two or more of her servants; she will probably hire you, since domestic service is the scarcest commodity on the Moon. If not, a variation will be arranged for you.

'When you are inside her dome, you'll manoeuvre yourselves into positions to carry out your assignments. When both of you are so placed, you will carry out procedures one and two with speed.

'A person named McGinty, already inside her dome, will help you in communication. He is not one of us but is our agent, a telepath. His ability does not extend past that. Your communication hook up will probably be, Gail to McGinty by telepathy, McGinty to Joe by concealed radio.'

Joe glanced at Gail; it was the first that he had known that she was a telepath. Baldwin went on, 'Gail will kill Mrs Keithley; Joe will break into the housing and destroy the circuits. Are you ready to go?'

Joe was about to suggest swapping the assignments when Gail answered, 'Ready'; he echoed her.

'Good. Joe, you will carry your assumed I.Q. at about 85, Gail at 95; she will appear to be the dominant member of a married couple –' Gail grinned at Joe. '– but you, Joe, will be in charge. Your personalities and histories are now being made up and will be ready with your identifications. Let me say again that the greatest of speed is necessary; government security forces here may attempt a foolhardy attack on the New Age Hotel. We shall prevent or delay such efforts, but act with speed. Good luck.'

Operation Black Widow, first phase, went off as planned. Eleven days later Joe and Gail were inside Mrs Keithley's dome on the Moon and sharing a room in the servants' quarters. Gail glanced around when first they entered it and said in Speedtalk, 'Now you'll have to marry me; I'm compromised.'

'Shut that up, idiot! Someone might hear you.'

'Pooh! They'd just think I had asthma. Don't you think it's noble of me, Joe, to sacrifice my girlish reputation for home and country?'

'What reputation?'

'Come closer so I can slug you.'

Even the servants' quarters were luxurious. The dome was a sybarite's dream. The floor of it was gardened in real beauty save where Mrs Keithley's mansion stood. Opposite it, across a little lake – certainly the only lake on the Moon – was the building housing the circuits; it was disguised as a little Doric Grecian shrine.

The dome itself was edge-lighted fifteen hours out of each twenty-four, shutting out the black sky and the harsh stars. At 'night' the lighting was gradually withdrawn.

McGinty was a gardener and obviously enjoyed his work. Gail established contact with him, got out of him what little he knew. Joe left him alone save for contacts in character.

There was a staff of over two hundred, having its own social hierarchy, from engineers for dome and equipment, Mrs Keithley's private pilot, and so on down to gardeners' helpers. Joe and Gail were midway, being inside servants. Gail made herself popular as the harmlessly flirtatious but always helpful and sympathetic wife of a meek and older husband. She had been a beauty parlour operator, so it seemed, before she 'married' and had great skill in massaging aching backs and stiff necks, relieving headaches and inducing sleep. She was always ready to demonstrate.

Her duties as a maid had not yet brought her into close contact with their employer. Joe, however, had acquired the job of removing all potted plants to the 'outdoors' during 'night'; Mrs Keithley, according to Mr James, the butler, believed that plants should be outdoors at 'night.' Joe was thus in a position to get outside the house when the dome was dark; he had already reached the point when the night guard at the Grecian temple would sometimes got Joe to 'jigger' for him while the guard snatched a forbidden cigarette.

McGinty had been able to supply one more important fact: in addition to the guard at the temple building, and the locks and armour plate of the building itself, the arming circuit was booby-trapped. Even if it were inoperative as an arming circuit for the 'Nova' bomb on Earth, it itself would blow up if tampered with. Gail and Joe discussed it in their room, Gail sitting on his lap like an affectionate wife, her lips close to his left ear. 'Perhaps you could wreck it from the door, without exposing yourself.'

"I've got to be sure. There is certainly some way of switching that gimmick off. She has to provide for possible repairs or replacements.'

'Where would it be?'

'Just one place that matches the pattern of the rest of her planning. Right under her hand, along with the disarming switch and the trigger switch.' He rubbed his other ear; it contained his short-range radio hook-up to McGinty and itched almost constantly.

'Hmm – then there's just one thing to be done; I'll have to wring it out of her before I kill her.'

'We'll see.'

Just before dinner the following 'evening' she found him in their room. 'It worked, Joe, it worked!'

'What worked?'

'She fell for the bait. She heard from her secretary about my skill as a masseuse; I was ordered up for a demonstration this afternoon. Now I am under strict instructions to come to her tonight and rub her to sleep.'

'It's tonight, then.'

McGinty waited in his room, behind a locked door. Joe stalled in the black hall, spinning out endlessly a dull tale to Mr James.

A voice in his ear said, 'She's in *her* room now.'

'– and that's how my brother got married to two women at once,' Joe concluded. 'Sheer bad luck. I better get these plants outside before the missus happens to ask about 'em.'

'I suppose you had. Goodnight.'

'Goodnight, Mr James.' He picked up two of the pots and waddled out.

He put them down outside and heard, 'She says she's started the massage. She's spotted the radio switching unit; it's on the belt that the old gal keeps at her bedside table when she's not wearing it.'

'Tell her to kill her and grab it.'

'She says she wants to make her tell how to unswitch the booby-trap gimmick first.'

'Tell her not to delay.'

Suddenly inside his head, clear and sweet as a bell as if they were her own spoken tones, he heard her. – *Joe, I can hear you. Can you hear me*?

– *Yes, yes!* Aloud he added, 'Stand by the phones anyhow, Mac.'

– *It won't be long. I have her in intense pain; she'll crack soon.*

– *Hurt her plenty!* He began to run towards the temple building. – *Gail, are you still shopping for a husband?* ...

– *I've found him.*

– *Marry me and I'll beat you every Saturday night.*

– *The man who can beat me hasn't been born.*

– *I'd like to try.* He slowed down before he came near the guard's station. 'Hi, Jim!'

– *It's a deal.*

'Well, if it taint Joey boy! Got a match?'

'Here.' He reached out a hand – then, as the guard fell, he eased him to the ground and made sure that he would stay out. – *Gail! It's got to be now!*

The voice in his head came back in great consternation: – *Joe! She was too tough, she wouldn't crack. She's dead!*

– *Good! Get that belt, break the arming circuit, then see what else you can find. I'm going to break in.*

He went towards the door of the temple.

– *It's disarmed, Joe. I could spot it; it has a time set*

on it. *I can't tell about the others; they aren't marked and they all look alike.*

He took from his pocket a small item provided by Baldwin's careful planning. – *Twist them all from where they are to the other way. You'll probably hit it.*

– *Oh, Joe, I hope so!*

He had placed the item against the lock; the metal around it turned red and now was melting away. An alarm clanged somewhere.

Gail's voice came again in his head; there was urgency in it but no fear: – *Joe! they're beating on the door. I'm trapped.*

– *McGinty! be our witness! He* went on: *I, Joseph, take thee, Gail, to be my lawfully wedded wife –*

He was answered in tranquil rhythm: – *I, Gail, take thee, Joseph, to be my lawfully wedded husband –*

– *To have and to hold,* he went on.

– *To have and to hold, my beloved!*

– *For better, for worse –*

–*for better, for worse –*Her voice in his head was singing. – *Till death do us part. I've got it open, darling; I am going in.*

– *Till death do us part! They are breaking down the bedroom door, Joseph, my dearest.*

– *Hang on! I'm almost through here.*

– *They have broken it down, Joe. They are coming towards me. Goodbye, my darling! I am very happy.* Abruptly her 'voice' stopped.

He was facing the box that housed the disarming circuit, alarms clanging in his ears; he took from his pocket another gadget and tried it.

The blast that shattered the box caught him full in the chest.

The letters on the metal marker read:

TO THE MEMORY OF
MR AND MRS JOSEPH GREENE
WHO, NEAR THIS SPOT,
DIED FOR ALL THEIR FELLOW MEN

Elsewhen

EXCERPT from the *Evening Standard:*

SOUGHT SAVANT EVADES POLICE

CITY HALL SCANDAL LOOMS

Professor Arthur Frost, wanted for questioning in connection with the mysterious disappearance from his home of five of his students, escaped today from under the noses of a squad of police sent to arrest him. Police Sergeant Izowiski claimed that Frost disappeared from the interior of the Black Maria under conditions which leave the police puzzled. District Attorney Karnes labelled Izowski's story as preposterous and promised the fullest possible investigation.

"But, Chief, I didn't leave him alone for a second!

'Nuts! ' answered the Chief of Police. 'You claim you put Frost in the wagon, stopped with one foot on the tailboard to write in your notebook, and when you looked up he was gone. D'yuh expect the Grand Jury to believe that? D'yuh expect *me* to believe that?'

'Honest, Chief,' protested Izowski, 'I just stopped to write down –'

'Write down what?'

'Something he said. I said to him. "Look, Doc, why don't you tell us where you hid 'em. You know we're bound to dig 'em up in time." And he just give me a funny far-away look, and says "Time – ah, time . . . yes, you could dig them up, in Time." I thought it was an important admission and stops to write it down. But I was standing in the only door he could use to get out

89

of the wagon, you know, I ain't little; I kinda fill up a door.'

'That's all you do,' commented the Chief bitterly. 'Izowski, you were either drunk, or crazy – or somebody got to you. The way you tell it, it's impossible!'

Izowski was honest, nor was he drunk, nor crazy.

Four days earlier Doctor Frost's class in speculative metaphysics had met as usual for their Friday evening seminar at the professor's home. Frost was saying. 'And why not? Why shouldn't time be a fifth as well as a fourth dimension?'

Howard Jenkins, a hard-headed engineering student, answered, 'No harm in speculating, I suppose, but the question is meaningless.'

'Why?' Frost's tones were deceptively mild.

'No question is meaningless,' interrupted Helen Fisher.

'Oh, yeah? How high is up?'

'Let him answer,' meditated Frost.

'I will,' agreed Jenkins. 'Human beings are constituted to perceive three spatial dimensions and one time dimension. Whether there are more of either is meaningless to us for there is no possible way for us to know – *ever*. Such speculation is a harmless waste of time.'

'So?' said Frost. 'Ever run across J. W. Dunne's theory of serial universe with serial time? And he's an engineer, like yourself. And don't forget Ouspensky. He regarded time as multi-dimensional.'

'Just a second, Professor,' put in Robert Monroe. 'I've seen their writings – but I still think Jenkins offered a legitimate objection. How can the question mean anything to us if we aren't built to perceive more dimensions? It's like in mathematics – you can invent any mathematics you like, on any set of axioms, but unless it can be used to describe some sort of phenomena, it's just so much hot air.'

'Fairly put,' conceded Frost. 'I'll give a fair answer. Scientific belief is based on observation, either one's own or that of a competent observer. I believe in a two-dimensional time because I have actually observed it.'

The clock ticked on for several seconds.

Jenkins said, 'But that is impossible, Professor. You aren't built to observe two time dimensions.'

'Easy, there . . .' answered Frost. 'I am built to perceive them *one at a time* – and so are you. I'll tell you about it, but before I do so, I must explain the theory of time I was forced to evolve in order to account for my experience. Most people think of time as a track that they run on from birth to death as inexorably as a train follows its rails – they feel instinctively that time follows a straight line, the past lying behind, the future lying in front. Now I have reason to believe – to know – that time is analogous to a surface rather than a line, and a rolling hilly surface at that. Think of this track we follow over the surface of time as a winding road cut through hills. Every little way the road branches and the branches follow side canyons. At these branches the crucial decisions of your life take place. You can turn right or left into entirely different futures. Occasionally there is a switchback where one can scramble up or down a bank and skip over a few thousand or million years – if you don't have your eyes so fixed on the road that you miss the short cut.

'Once in a while another road crosses yours. Neither its past nor its furture has any connection whatsoever with the world we know. If you happened to take that turn you might find yourself on another planet in another space-time with nothing left of you or your world but the continuity of your ego.

'Or, if you have the necessary intellectual strength and courage, you may leave the roads, or paths of high probability, and strike out over the hills of possible time, cutting through the roads as you come to them, following them for a little way, even following them backwards, with the past *ahead* of you, and the future *behind* you. Or you might roam around the hilltops doing nothing but the extremely improbable. I cannot imagine what that would be like – perhaps a bit like Alice-through-the-Looking-Glass.

'Now as to my evidence – When I was eighteen I had a decision to make. My father suffered financial reverses and I decided to quit college. Eventually I went into business for myself, and, to make a long story short, in nineteen-fifty-eight I was convicted of fraud and went to prison.'

Martha Ross interrupted. 'Nineteen-fifty-eight, Doctor? You mean forty-eight?'

'No, Miss Ross. I am speaking of events that did not take place on this time track.'

'Oh!' She looked blank, then muttered, 'With the Lord all things are possible.'

'While in prison I had time to regret my mistakes. I realised that I had never been cut out for a business career, and I earnestly wished that I had stayed in school many years before. Prison has a peculiar effect on a man's mind. I drifted further and further away from reality, and lived more and more in an introspective world of my own. One night, in a way not then clear to me, my ego left my cell, went back along the time track, and I awoke in my room at my college fraternity house.

'This time I was wiser – Instead of leaving school, I found part-time work, graduated, continued as a graduate fellow, and eventually arrived where you now see me.' He paused and glanced around.

'Doctor,' asked young Monroe, 'can you give us any idea as to how the stunt was done?'

'Yes, I can,' Frost assented. 'I worked on that problem for many years, trying to recapture the conditions. Recently I have succeeded and have made several excursions into possibility.'

Up to this time the third woman, Estelle Martin, had made no comment, although she had listened with close attention. Now she leaned forward and spoke in an intense whisper.

'Tell us how, Professor Frost! '

'The means are simple. The key lies in convincing the subconscious mind that it can be done –'

'Then the Berkeleian idealism is proved! '

'In a way, Miss Martin. To one who believes in Bishop Berkeley's philosophy the infinite possibilities of two-dimensional time offer proof that the mind creates its own world, but a Spencerian determinist, such as good friend Howard Jenkins, would never leave the road of maximum probability. To him the world would be mechanistic and real. An orthodox free-will Christian, such as Miss Ross, would have her choice of several of the side roads, but would probably remain in a physical environment similar to Howard's.

'I have perfected a technique which will enable others to travel about in the pattern of times as I have done. I have the apparatus ready and any who wish can try it. That is the real reason why these Friday evening meetings have been held in my home – so that when the time came you all might try it, if you wished.' He got up and went to a cabinet at the end of the room.

'You mean we could go tonight, Doctor?'

'Yes, indeed. The process is one of hypnotism and suggestion. Neither are necessary, but that is the quickest way of teaching the sub-conscious to break out of its groove and go where it pleases. I use a revolving ball to tire the conscious mind into hypnosis. During that period the subject listens to a recording which suggests the time-road to be followed, whereupon he does. It is as simple as that. Do any of you care to try it?'

'Is it likely to be dangerous, Doctor?'

He shrugged his shoulders. 'The process isn't – just a deep sleep and a phonograph record. But the world of the time track you visit will be as real as the world of this time track. You are all over twenty-one. I am not urging you, I am merely offering you the opportunity.'

Monroe stood up. 'I'm going, Doctor.'

'Good! Sit here and use these earphones. Anyone else?'

'Count me in.' It was Helen Fisher.

Estelle Martin joined them. Howard Jenkins went hastily to her side. 'Are you going to try this business?'

'Most certainly.'

He turned to Frost. 'I'm in, Doc.'

Martha Ross finally joined the others. Frost seated them where they could wear the earphones and then asked.

'You will remember the different types of things you could do; branch off into a different world, skip over into the past or the future, or cut straight through the maze of probable tracks on a path of extreme improbability. I have records for all of those.'

Monroe was first again. 'I'll take a right angle turn and a brand new world.'

Estelle did not hesitate. 'I want to – how did you put it? – climb up a bank to a higher road somewhere in the future.'

'I'll try that, too.' It was Jenkins.

'I'll take the remote-possibilities track,' put in Helen Fisher.

'That takes care of everybody but Miss Ross,' commented the Professor. 'I'm afraid you will have to take a branch path in probability. Does that suit you?'

She nodded. 'I was going to ask for it.'

'That's fine. All of these records contain the suggestion for you to return to this room two hours from now, figured along this time track. Put on your earphones. The records run thirty minutes. I'll start them and the ball together.'

He swung a glittering many-faceted sphere from a hook in the ceiling, started it whirling, and turned a small spotlight on it. Then he turned off the other lights, and started all the records by throwing a master switch. The scintillating ball twirled round and round, slowed and reversed and twirled back again. Doctor Frost turned his eyes away to keep from being fascinated by it. Presently he slipped out into the hall for a smoke. Half an hour passed and there came the single note of a gong. He hurried back and switched on the light.

Four of the five had disappeared.

'The remaining figure was Howard Jenkins, who opened his eyes and blinked at the light. 'Well, Doctor, I guess it didn't work.'

The Doctor raised his eyebrows. 'No? Look around you.'

The younger man glanced about him. 'Where are the others?'

'Where? Anywhere,' replied Frost, with a shrug, 'and any-*when*.'

Jenkins jerked off his earphone and jumped to his feet. 'Doctor, *what have you done to Estelle?*'

Frost gently disengaged a hand from his sleeve. 'I haven't done anything. Howard. She's out on another time track.'

'But I meant to go with her! '

'And I tried to send you with her.'

'But why didn't I go?'

'I can't say – probably the suggestion wasn't strong to overcome your scepticism. But don't be alarmed, son – We expect her back in a couple of hours, you know.'

'Don't be alarmed! – that's easy to say. I didn't want her to try this damn fool stunt in the first place, but I knew I couldn't change her mind, so I wanted to go along to look out for her – she so impractical! But see here, Doc – where are their bodies? I thought we would just stay here in the room in a trance.'

'Apparently you didn't understand me. These other time tracks are real, as real as this one we are in. Their whole beings have gone off on the other tracks, as if they had turned down a side street.'

'But that's impossible – it contradicts the law of the conservation of energy! '

'You must recognise a fact when you see one – they are gone. Besides, it doesn't contradict the law; it simply extends it to include the total universe.'

Jenkins rubbed a hand over his face. 'I suppose so. But in that case, anything can happen to her – she could even be *killed* out there. And I can't do a damn thing about it. Oh, I wish we had never seen this damned seminar! '

The Professor placed an arm around his shoulders. 'Since you can't help her, why not calm down? Besides, you have no reason to believe that she is in any danger. Why borrow trouble? Let's go out to the kitchen and open a bottle of beer while we wait for them.' He gently urged him towards the door.

After a couple of beers and a few cigarettes, Jenkins was somewhat calmed down. The Professor made conversation.

'How did you happen to sign up for this course, Howard?'

'It was the only course I could take with Estelle.'

'I thought so. I let you take it for reasons of my own. I knew you weren't interested in speculative philosophy, but I thought that your hard-headed materialism would hold down some of the loose thinking that is likely to go on in such a class. You've been a help to me. Take Helen Fisher for example. She is prone to reason brilliantly from insufficient data. You help to keep her down to earth.'

'To be frank, Doctor Frost, I could never see the need for all this high-falutin discussion. I like facts.'

'But you engineers are as bad as metaphysicians – you ignore any fact that you can't weigh in scales. If you can't bite it, it's not real. You believe in a mechanistic, deterministic universe, and ignore the facts of human consciousness, human will, and human freedom of choice – facts that you have directly experienced.'

'But those things can be explained in terms of reflexes.'

The Professor spread his hands. 'You sound just like Martha Ross – she can explain anything in terms of Biblebelt fundamentalism. Why don't both of you admit that there are a few things that you don't understand?'

He paused and cocked his head. 'Did you hear something?'

'I think I did.'

'Let's check. It's early, but perhaps one of them is back.'

They hurried to the study, where they were confronted by an incredible and awe-inspiring sight.

Floating in the air near the fireplace was a figure robed in white and shining with a soft mother-of-pearl radiance. While they stood hesitant at the door, the figure turned its face to them and they saw it had the face of Martha Ross, cleansed and purified to an unhuman majesty. Then it spoke.

'Peace be unto you, my brothers.' A wave of peace and loving-kindness flowed over them like a mother's blessing. The figure approached them, and they saw, curving from its shoulders, the long, white, sweeping wings of a classical angel. Frost cursed under his breath in a dispassionate monotone.

'Do not be afraid. I have come back, as you asked me to. To explain and to help you.'

The Doctor found his voice. 'Are you Martha Ross?'

'I answer to that name.'

'What happened after you put on the earphones?'

'Nothing. I slept for a while. When I woke, I went home.'

'Nothing else? How do you explain your appearance?'

'My appearance is what you earthly children expect of the Lord's Redeemed. In the course of time I served as a missionary in South America. There it was required of me that I give up my mortal life in the service of the Lord. And so I entered the Eternal City.'

'You went to Heaven?'

'These many eons I have sat at the foot of the Golden Throne and sung hosannas to His name.'

Jenkins interrupted them. 'Tell me, Martha – or Saint Martha – *where is Estelle?* Have you seen her?'

The figure turned slowly and faced him. 'Fear not.'

'But tell me where she is!'

'It is not needful.'

'That's no help,' he answered bitterly.

'I will help you. Listen to me; Love the Lord thy God with all thy heart, and Love thy neighbours as thyself. That is all you need to know.'

Howard remained silent, at a loss for an answer, but unsatisfied. Presently the figure spoke again. 'I must go. God's blessing on you.' It flickered and was gone.

The Professor touched the young man's arm. 'Let's get some fresh air.' He led Jenkins, mute and unresisting, out into the garden. They walked for some minutes in silence. Finally Howard asked a question.

'Did we see an angle in there?'

'I think so, Howard.'

'But that's insane!'

'There are millions of people who wouldn't think so – unusual certainly, but not insane.'

'But it's contrary to all modern beliefs – Heaven – Hell – a personal God – Resurrection. Everything I've believed in must be wrong, or I've gone screwy.'

'Not necessarily – not even probably. I doubt very much if you will ever see Heaven or Hell. You'll follow a time track in accordance with your nature.'

'But she seemed *real*.'

'She *was* real. I suspect that the conventional hereafter is real to any one who believes in it wholeheartedly, as Martha evidently did, but I expect you to follow a pattern in accordance with the beliefs of an agnostic – except in one respect; when you die, you won't die all over, no matter how intensely you may claim to expect to. *It is an emotional impossibility for any man to believe in his own death.* That sort of self-annihilation can't be done. You'll have a hereafter, but it will be one appropriate to a materialist.'

But Howard was not listening. He pulled at his under lip and frowned. 'Say, Doc, why wouldn't Martha tell me what happened to Estelle? That was a dirty trick.'

'I doubt if she knew, my boy. Martha followed a time track only slightly different from that we are in; Estelle chose to explore one far in the past, or in the distant future. For all practical purposes, each is non-existent to the other.'

They heard a call from the house, a clear contralto voice, 'Doctor! Doctor Frost! '

Jenkins whirled around 'That's Estelle! ' They ran back into the house, the Doctor endeavouring manfully to keep up.

But it was not Estelle. Standing in the hallway was Helen Fisher, her sweater torn and dirty, her stockings missing, and a barely-healed scar puckering one cheek. Frost stopped and surveyed her. 'Are you all right, child?' he demanded.

She grinned boyishly. 'I'm okay. You should see the other guy.'

'Tell us about it.'

'In a minute. How about a cup of coffee for the prodigal? And I wouldn't turn up my nose at scrambled eggs and some – lots – of toast. Meals are inclined to be irregular where I've been.'

'Yes, indeed. Right away,' answered Frost, 'but where *have* you been?'

'Let a gal eat, please,' she begged. 'I won't hold out on you. What is Howard looking so sour about?'

The Professor whispered an explanation. She gave Jenkins a compassionate glance. 'Oh, she hasn't? I thought I'd be the last man in: I was away so long. What day is this?'

Frost glanced at his wrist watch. 'You're right on time; it's just eleven o'clock.'

'The hell you say! Oh, excuse me, Doctor. "Curiouser and curiouser, said Alice." All in a couple of hours. Just for the record, I was gone several weeks at least.'

When her third cup of coffee had washed down the last of the toast, she began:

'When I woke up I was falling upstairs – through a

nightmare, several nightmares. Don't ask me to describe *that* – nobody could. That went on for a week, maybe, then things started to come into focus. I don't know in just what order things happened, but when I started to notice clearly I was standing in a little barren valley. It was cold, and the air was thin and acrid. It burned my throat. There were two suns in the sky, one big and reddish, the other smaller and too bright to look at.'

'Two suns!' exclaimed Howard. 'That's not possible – binary stars don't have planets.'

She looked at him. 'Have it your own way – I was *there*. Just as I was taking this all in, something whizzed overhead and I ducked. That was the last I saw of *that* place.

'I slowed down next back on earth – at least it looked like it – and in a city. It was a big and complicated city. I was in trafficway with a lot of fast-moving traffic. I stepped out and tried to flag one of the vehicles – a long crawling caterpillar thing with about fifty wheels – when I caught sight of what was driving it and dodged back in a hurry. It wasn't a man and it wasn't an animal either – not one I've ever seen or heard of. It wasn't a bird, or a fish, nor an insect. The god that thought up the inhabitants of that city doesn't deserve worship. I don't know what they were, but they crawled and they crept and they *stank*. Ugh!

'I slunk around holes in that place,' she continued, 'for a couple of weeks before I recovered the trick of jumping the time track. I was desperate, for I thought that the suggestion to return to now hadn't worked. I couldn't find much to eat and I was light-headed part of the time. I drank out of what I suspect was their drainage system, but there was nobody to ask and I didn't want to know. I was thirsty.'

'Did you see any human beings?'

'I'm not sure. I saw some shapes that might have been men squatting in a circle down in the tunnels under the city, but something frightened them, and they scurried away before I could get close enough to look.'

'What else happened there?'

'Nothing. I found the trick again that same night and got away from there as fast as I could. I am afraid I lost the scientific spirit, Professor – I didn't care how the other half lived.

'This time I had better luck. I was on earth again. but in pleasant rolling hills, like the Blue Ridge Mountains. It was summer, and very lovely. I found a little stream and took off my clothes and bathed. It was wonderful. After I had found some ripe berries, I lay down in the sun and went to sleep.

'I woke wide awake with a start. Someone was bending over me. It was a man, but no beauty. He was a Neanderthal. I should have run, but I tried to grab my clothes first, so he grabbed me. I was led back in to camp, a Sabine woman, with my new spring sports outfit tucked fetchingly under one arm.

'I wasn't so bad off. It was the Old Man who had found me, and he seemed to regard me as a strange pet, about on a par with the dogs that snarled around the bone heap, rather than as a member of his harem. I fed well enough, if you aren't fussy – I wasn't fussy after living in the bowels of that awful city.

'The Neanderthal isn't a bad fellow at heart, rather good-natured, although inclined to play rough. That's how I got this.' She fingered the scar on her cheek. 'I had about decided to stay a while and study them when one day I made a mistake. It was a chilly morning, and I put on my clothes for the first time since I had arrived. One of the young bucks saw me, and I guessed it aroused his romantic nature. The Old Man was away at the time and there was no one to stop him.

'He grabbed me before I knew what was happening and tried to show his affection. Have you ever been nuzzled by a cave man, Howard? They have halitosis, not to mention B.O. I was too startled to concentrate on the time trick, or else I would have slipped right out into

101

space-time and left him clutching air.'

Doctor Frost was aghast. 'Dear God, child ! What did you do?'

'I finally showed him a ju jitsu trick I learned in Phys. Ed. II, then I ran like hell and shinned up a tree. I counted up to a hundred and tried to be calm. Pretty soon I was shooting upstairs in a nightmare again and very happy to be doing it.'

'Then you came back here?'

'Not by a whole lot – worse luck! I landed in this present all right, and apparently along this time dimension, but there was plenty that was wrong about it. I was standing on the south side of Forty-Second Street in New York. I knew where I was for the first thing I noticed was the big lighted letters that chase around the TIMES building and spell out news flashes. It was running backwards. I was trying to figure out "DETROIT BEAT TO HITS NINE GETS YANKEES" when I saw two cops running as hard as they could – backwards, away from.'

Doctor Frost smothered an ejaculation. 'What did you say?'

'Reversed entropy – you entered the track backwards – your time arrow was pointing backwards.'

'I figured that out, when I had time to think about it. Just then I was too busy. I was in a clearing in the crowd, but the ring of people was closing in on me, all running backwards. The cops disappeared in the crowd, and the crowd ran right up to me, stopped, and started to scream. Just as that happened, the traffic lights changed, cars charged out from both directions, driving backwards. It was too much for little Helen. I fainted.

'Following that I seemed to slant through a lot of places –'

'Just a second,' Howard interrupted, 'just what happened before that – I thought I savvied entropy, but that got me licked.'

'Well,' explained Frost, 'the easiest way to explain it is to say that she was travelling backwards in time. Her

102

future was their past, and vice versa. I'm glad she got out in a hurry. I'm not sure that human metabolism can be maintained in such conditions.'

'Hmm – Go ahead, Helen.'

'This slanting through the axes would have been startling, if I hadn't been emotionally exhausted. I sat back and watched it, like a movie. I think Salvador Dali wrote the script. I saw landscapes heave and shift like a stormy sea. People melted into plants – I think my own body changed at times, but I can't be sure. Once I found myself in a place that was all *insides*, instead of outsides, Some of the things we'll skip – I don't believe them myself.

'Then I slowed down in a place that must have had an extra spatial dimension. Everything looked three dimensional to me, but they changed their shapes when I *thought* about them. I found I could look inside solid objects simply by wanting to. When I tired of prying into the intimate secrets of rocks and plants, I took a look at myself, and it worked just as well. I know more about anatomy and physiology now than an M.D. It's fun to watch your heart beat – kind o'cute.

'But my appendix was swollen and inflamed. I found I could reach it and touch it – it was tender. I've had trouble with it so I decided to perform an emergency operation. I nipped it off with my nails. It didn't hurt at all, bled a couple of drops and closed right up.

'Good Heavens, child! You might have gotten peritonitis and died.'

'I don't think so. I believe that ultra-violet was pouring all through me and killing the bugs. I had a fever for a while, but I think what caused it was a bad case of internal sunburn.

'I forgot to mention that I couldn't walk around in this place, for I couldn't seem to touch anything but myself. I sliced right through anything I tried to get a purchase on. Pretty soon I quit trying and relaxed. It was comfortable and I went into a warm happy dope, like a hibernating bear.

'After a long time – a long, long time, I went sound asleep and came to in your big easy chair. That's all.'

Helen answered Howard's anxious inquiries by telling him that she had seen nothing of Estelle. 'But why don't you calm down and wait? She isn't really overdue.'

They were interrupted by the opening of the door from the hallway. A short wiry figure in a hooded brown tunic and tight brown breeches strode into the room.

'Where's Doctor Frost? Oh – Doctor, I need help!'

It was Monroe, but changed almost beyond recognition. He had been short and slender before, but now barely five feet tall, and stocky, with powerful shoulder muscles. The brown costume with its peaked hood, or helmet, gave him a strong resemblance to the popular notion of gnome.

Frost hurried to him. 'What is it, Robert. How can I help?'

'This first.' Monroe hunched forward for inspection of his left upper arm. The fabric was tattered and charred, exposing an ugly burn. 'He just grazed me, but it had better be fixed, if I am to save the arm.'

Frost examined it without touching it. 'We must rush you to a hospital.'

'No time. I've got to get back. They need me – and the help I can bring.'

The Doctor shook his head. 'You've got to have treatment, Bob. Even if there is a strong need for you to get back wherever you have been, you are in a different time track now. Time lost here isn't necessarily lost there.'

Monroe cut him short. 'I think this world and my world have connected time rates. I must hurry.'

Helen Fisher placed herself between them. 'Let me see that arm. Bob. Hm – pretty nasty, but I think I can fix it. Professor, put a kettle on the fire with about a cup of water in it. As soon as it boils, chuck in a handful of tea leaves.'

She rummaged through the kitchen cutlery drawer,

found a pair of shears, and did a neat job of cutting away the sleeve and cleaning the burned flesh for dressing. Monroe talked as she worked.

'Howard, I want you to do me a favour. Get a pencil and paper and take down a list. I want a flock of things to take back – all of them things that you can pick up at the fraternity house. You'll have to go for me – I'd be thrown out with my present appearance – What's the matter? Don't you want to?'

Helen hurriedly explained Howard's preoccupation. He listened sympathetically. 'Oh! Say, that's tough lines, old man.' His brow wrinkled. 'But look – You can't do Estelle any good by waiting here, and I really do need your help for the next half hour. Will you do it?'

Jenkins reluctantly agreed. Monroe continued.

'Fine! I do appreciate it. Go to my room first and gather up my reference books on math – also my slide rule. You'll find an India-paper radio manual, too. I want that. And I want your twenty inch-long-log duplex slide rule as well. You can have my Rabelais and the *Droll Stories.* I want your *Marks' Mechanical Engineers' Handbook,* and any other technical reference books that you have and I haven't. Take anything you like in exchange.

'Then go up to Stinky Beanfield's room, and get his *Military Engineer's Handbook,* his *Chemical Warfare,* and hes texts on ballistics and ordnances. Yes, and Miller's *Chemistry of Explosives,* if he has one. If not, pick up one from some other of the R.O.T.C. boys; it's important.' Helen was deftly applying a poultice to his arm. He winced as the tea leaves, still warm, touched his seared flesh, but went ahead.

'Stinky keeps his service automatic in his upper bureau drawer. Swipe it, or talk him out of it. Bring as much ammunition as you can find – I'll write out a bill of sale for my car for you to leave for him. Now get going. I'll tell Doc all about it, and he can tell you later. Here. Take my car.' He fumbled at his thigh, then looked annoyed. 'Cripes! I don't have my keys.'

105

Helen came to the rescue. 'Take mine. The keys are in my bag on the hall table.'

Howard got up. 'Okay, I'll do my damndest. If I get flung in the can, bring me cigarettes.' He went out.

Helen put the finishing touches on the bandages. 'There! I think that will do. How does it feel?'

He flexed his arm cautiously. 'Okay. It's a neat job, kid. It takes the sting out.'

'I believe it will heal if you keep tannin solution on it. Can you get tea leaves where you are going?'

'Yes, and tannic acid, too. I'll be all right. Now you deserve an explanation. Professor, do you have a cigarette on you? I could use some of that coffee, too.

'Surely, Robert.' Frost hastened to serve him.

'Monroe accepted a light and began.

'It's all pretty cock-eyed. When I came out of the sleep, I found myself dressed as I am now looking as I now look, marching down a long, deep fosse. I was one of a column of threes in a military detachment. The odd part about it is that I felt perfectly natural. I knew where I was and why I was there – and who I was. I don't mean Robert Monroe; my name over there is Igor.' Monroe pronounced the guttural deep in his throat and trilled the 'r'. 'I hadn't forgotten Monroe, it was more as if I had suddenly remembered him. I had one identity and two pasts. It was something like waking up from a clearly remembred dream, only the dream was perfectly real. I knew Monroe was real, just as I knew Igor was real.

'My world was much like earth; a bit smaller, but much the same surface gravity. Men like myself are the dominant race, and we are about as civilised as you folks, but our culture has followed a difficult course. We live underground about half the time. Our homes are there and a lot of our industry, you see it's warm underground in our world, and not entirely dark. There is a mild radioactivity; it doesn't harm us.

'Nevertheless we are a surface-evolved race, and can't

106

be healthy nor happy if we stay underground all the time. Now there is a war on and we've been driven underground for eight or nine earth months. The war is going against us. As it stands now, we have lost control of the surface and my race is being reduced to the status of ! unted vermin.

'You see, we aren't fighting human beings. I don't know just what it is we are fighting – maybe beings from outer space. We don't know. They attacked us several places at once from great flying rings the like of which we had never seen. They burned us down without warning. Many of us escaped underground where they haven't followed us. They don't operate at night either – seem to need sunlight to be active. So it's a stalemate – or was until they started gassing our tunnels.

'We've never captured one and consequently don't know what makes them tick. We examined a ring that crashed, but didn't learn much. There was nothing inside that even vaguely resembled animal life, nor was there anything to support animal life. I mean there were no food supplies, nor sanitary arrangements. Opinion is divided between the idea that the enemy are some sort of non-protoplasmic intelligence, perhaps force patterns, or something equally odd.

'Our principal weapon is a beam which creates a stasis in the ether, and freezes 'em solid. Or rather it should, but it will destroy all life and prevent molar action – but the rings are simply put temporarily out of control. Unless we can keep a beam on a ring right to the moment it crashes, it recovers and gets away. Then its pals come and burn out our position.

'We've had better luck with mining their surface camps, and blowing them up at night. We're accomplished sappers, of course. But we need better weapons. That's what I sent Howard after. I've got two ideas. If the enemy are simply some sort of intelligent force patterns, or something like that, radio may be the answer. We might be able to fill up the ether with static and jam them right out of existence. If they are too tough for that, perhaps some good old-fashioned anti-aircraft fire might make them say "Uncle." In any case there is a lot of technology here that we don't have, and which may have the answer. I wish I had time to pass on some of our stuff in return for what I'm taking with me.'

'You are determined to go back, Robert?'

'Certainly. It's where I belong. I've no family here. I don't know how to make you see it, Doc, but those are my people – that is my world. I suppose if conditions were reversed, I'd feel differently.'

'I see,' said Helen, 'you're fighting for the wife and kids.'

He turned a weary face toward her. 'Not exactly. I'm a bachelor over there, but I do have a family to think about; my sister is in command of the attack until I'm in. Oh, yes, the women are in it – they're little and tough, like you, Helen.'

She touched his arm lightly. 'How did you pick up this?'

'That burn? You remember we were on the march. We were retreating down that ditch from a surface raid. I thought we had made good our escape when all of a sudden a ring swooped down on us. Most of the detachment scattered, but I'm a junior technician armed with the stasis ray. I tried to get my equipment unlimbered to fight back, but I was burned down before I could finish, Luckily it barely grazed me. Several of the others were fried. I don't know yet whether or not Sis got hers. That's one of the reasons why I'm in a hurry.

'One of the other techs who wasn't hit got his gear set up and covered our retreat. I was dragged underground and taken to a dressing station. The medicos were about to work on me when I passed out and came to in the Professor's study.'

The door bell rang and the Professor got up to answer it. Helen and Robert followed him. It was Howard, bearing spoils.

'Did you get everything?' Robert asked anxiously.

'I think so. Stinky was in, but I managed to borrow his books. The gun was harder, but I telephoned a friend of mine and had him call back and ask for Stinky. While he was out of the room, I lifted it. Now I'm a criminal – government property, too.'

'You're a pal, Howard. After you hear the explanation, you'll agree that it was worth doing. Won't he, Helen?'

'Absolutely!'

'Well, I hope you're right,' he answered dubiously. 'I brought along something else, just in case. Here it is.' He handed Robert a book.

'*Aerodynamics and Principles of Aircraft Construction*,' Robert read aloud. 'My God, yes! Thanks, Howard.'

In a few minutes, Monroe had his belongings assembled and fastened to his person. He had announced that he was ready when the Professor checked him.

'One moment, Robert. How do you know that these books will go with you?'

'Why not? That's why I'm fastening them to me.'

'Did your earthly clothing go through the first time?'

'No-o –' His brow furrowed. 'Good grief, Doc, what can I do? I couldn't possibly memorise what I need to know.'

'I don't know, son. Let's think about it a bit.' He broke off and stared at the ceiling. Helen touched his hand.

'Perhaps I can help, Professor.'

'In what way, Helen?'

'Apparently I don't metamorphose when I change time tracks. I had the same clothes with me everywhere I went. Why couldn't I ferry this stuff over for Bob?'

'No, I couldn't let you do that,' interposed Monroe. 'You might get killed or badly hurt.'

'I'll chance it.'

'I've got an idea,' put in Jenkins. 'Couldn't Doctor Frost set his instructions so that Helen would go over

109

and come right back? How about it, Doc?'

'Mmm, yes, Perhaps.' But Helen held up a hand.

'No good. The boodle might come bouncing back with me. I'll go over without any return instructions. I like the sound of this world of Bob's anyway. I may stay there. Cut out the chivalry, Bob. One of the things I liked about your world was the notion of treating men and women alike. Get unstuck from that stuff and start hanging it on me. I'm going.'

She looked like a Christmas tree when the dozen-odd books had been tied to various parts of her solid figure, the automatic pistol strapped on, and the two slide rules, one long and one short, stuck in the pistol belt.

Howard fondled the large slide rule before he fastened it on. 'Take good care of this slipstick, Bob,' he said, I gave up smoking for six months to pay for it.'

Frost seated the two side by side on the sofa in the study. Helen slipped a hand into Bob's. When the shining ball had been made to spin, Frost motioned for Jenkins to leave, closed the door after him and switched out the light. Then he started repeating hypnotic suggestions in a monotone.

Ten minutes later he felt a slight swish of air and ceased. He snapped the light switch. The sofa was empty, even of books.

Frost and Jenkins kept an uneasy vigi' while awaiting Estelle's return. Jenkins wandered nervously around the study, examining objects that didn't interest him and smoking countless cigarettes. The Professor sat quietly in his easy chair, simulating a freedom from anxiety that he did not feel. They conversed in a desultory fashion.

'One thing I don't see,' observed Jenkins, 'is why in the world Helen could go a dozen places and not change, and Bob goes just one place and comes back almost unrecognisable – shorter, heavier, decked out in outlandish clothes. What happened to his ordinary clothes anyhow? How do you explain those things, Professor?'

'Eh? I don't explain them – I merely observe them. I

think perhaps he changed, while Helen didn't, because Helen was just a visitor to the places she went to, whereas Monroe belonged over there – as witness he fitted into the pattern of the world. Perhaps the Great Architect intended for him to cross over.'

'Huh? Good heavens, Doctor, surely you don't believe in divine predestination!'

'Perhaps not in those terms. But, Howard, you mechanistic sceptics make me tired. Your naïve ability to believe that things "jest growed" approaches childishness. According to you a fortuitous accident of entropy produced Beethoven's Ninth Symphony.'

'I think that's unfair, Doctor. You certainly don't expect a man to believe in things that run contrary to his good sense without offering him any reasonable explanation.'

Frost snorted. 'I certainly do – if he has observed it with his own eyes and ears, or gets it from a source known to be credible. A fact doesn't have to be understood to be true. Sure, any reasonable mind wants explanations, but it's silly to reject facts that don't fit your philosophy.

'Now these events tonight, which you are so anxious to rationalise in orthodox terms, furnish a clue to a lot of things that scientists have been rejecting because they couldn't explain them. Have you ever heard the tale of the man who walked around the horses? No? Around 1810 Benjamin Bathurst, British Ambassador to Austria, arrived in his carriage at an inn in Perleberg, Germany. He had his valet and secretary with him. They drove into the lighted courtyard of the inn. Bathurst got out, and in the presence of bystanders and his two attaches, walked around the horses. He hasn't been seen since.

'Nobody knows. I think he was preoccupied and inadvertently wandered into another time track. But there are literally hundreds of similar cases, way too many to laugh off. The two-time-dimensions theory accounts for most of them. But I suspect that there are others as-yet-undreamed-of natural principles operating in some of the rejected cases.

Howard stopped pacing and pulled at his lower lip. 'Maybe so, Doctor. I'm too upset to think. Look here – it's one o'clock. Oughtn't she to be back by now?'

'I'm afraid so, son.'

'You mean she's not coming back.'

'It doesnt look like it.'

The younger man gave a broken cry and collapsed on the sofa. His shoulders heaved. Presently he calmed down a little. Frost saw his lips move and suspected that he was praying. Then he showed a drawn face to the Doctor.

'Isn't there *anything* we can do?'

'That's hard to answer, Howard. We don't know where she's gone; all we know is that she left here under hypnotic suggestion to cross over into some other loop of the past or future.'

'Can't we go after her the same way and trace her?'

'I don't know. I haven't had any experience with such a job.'

'I've got to do something or I'll go nuts.'

'Take it easy, son. Let me think about it.' He smoked in silence while Howard controlled an impulse to scream, break furniture, anything!

Frost knocked the ash off his cigar and placed it carefully in a tray. 'I can think of one chance. It's a remote one.'

'Anything!'

'I'm going to listen to the record that Estelle heard, and cross over. I'll do it wide awake, while concentrating in her. Perhaps I can establish some rapport, some extra-sensory connection, that will serve to guide me to her.' Frost went immediately about his preparations as he spoke. 'I want you to remain in the room when I go so that you will really believe that it can be done.

In silence Howard watched him don the headphones. The Professor stood still, eyes closed. He remained so for nearly fifteen minutes, then took a short step forward. The earphones clattered to the floor. He was gone.

Frost felt himself drift off into the timeless limbo which precedes transition. He noticed again that it was exactly like the floating sensation that ushers in normal sleep, and wondered idly, for the hundredth time, whether or not the dreams of sleep were real experiences. He was inclined to think they were. Then he recalled his mission with a guilty start, and concentrated hard on Estelle.

He was walking along a road, white in the sunshine. Before him were the gates of a city. The gateman stared at his odd attire, but let him pass. He hurried down the broad tree-lined avenue which (he knew) led from the space port to Capitol Hill. He turned aside into the Way of the Gods and continued until he reached the Grove of the Priestesses. There he found the house which he sought, its marble walls pink in the sun, its fountains tinkling in the morning breeze. He turned in.

The ancient janitor, nodding in the sun, admitted him to the house. The slender maidservant, barely nubile, ushered him into the inner chamber, where her mistress raised herself on one elbow and regarded her visitor through languid eyes. Frost addressed her.

'It is time to return, Estelle.'

Her eyebrows showed her surprise. 'You speak a strange and barbarous tongue, old man, and yet, here is a mystery, for I know it. What do you wish of me?'

Frost spoke impatiently. 'Estelle, I say it is time to return!'

'Return? What idle talk is this? Return where? And my name is Star-Light, not Ess Tell. Who are you, and from where do you come?' She searched his face, then pointed a slender finger at him. 'I know you now! You are out of my dreams. You were a Master and instructed me in the ancient wisdom.'

'Estelle, do you remember a youth in those dreams?'

'That odd name again! Yes, there was a youth. He

was sweet – sweet and straight and tall like pine on the mountain. I have dreamed of him often.' She swung about with a flash of long white limbs. 'What of this youth?'

'He waits for you. It is time to return.'

'Return! – There is no return to the place of dreams!'

'I can lead you there.'

'What blasphemy is this? Are you a priest, that you should practise magic? Why should a sacred courtesan go to the place of dreams?'

'There is no magic to it. He is heartsick at your loss. I will lead you back to him.'

She hesitated, doubt in her eyes, then she replied. 'Suppose you could; why should I leave my honourable sacred station for the cold nothingness of that dream?'

He answered her gently, 'What does your heart tell you, Estelle?'

She stared at him, eyes wide, and seemed about to burst into tears. Then she flung herself across the couch, and showed him her back. A muffled voice answered him.

'Be off with you! There is no youth, except in my dreams. I'll seek him there!'

She made no further reply to his importunities. Presently he ceased trying and left with a heavy heart.

Howard seized him by the arm as he returned. 'Well, Professor? Well? Did you find her?

Frost dropped wearily into his chair. 'Yes, I found her.'

'Was she all right? Why didn't she come back with you?'

'She was perfectly well, but I couldn't persuade her to return.'

Howard looked as if he had been slapped across the mouth. 'Didn't you tell her I wanted her to come back?'

'I did, but she didn't believe me.'

'Not believe you?'

'You see she's forgotten most of this life, Howard. She thinks you are simply a dream.'

'But that's not possible! '

Frost looked more weary than ever. 'Don't you think it is about time you stopped using that term, son?'

Instead of replying he answered, 'Doctor, you must take me to her! ' Frost looked dubious.

'Can't you do it?'

'Perhaps I could, if you have gotten over your disbelief, but still –'

'Disbelief! – I've been forced to believe. Let's get busy.'

Frost did not move. 'I'm not sure that I agree. Howard, conditions are quite different where Estelle has gone. It suits her, but I'm not sure that it would be a kindness to take you through to her.'

'Why not? Doesn't she want to see me?'

'Yes – I think she does. I'm sure she would welcome you, but conditions are very different.'

'I don't give a damn what the conditions are. Let's go.'

Frost got up. 'Very well. It shall be as you wish.'

He seated Jenkins in the easy chair and held the young man's eyes with his gaze. He spoke slowly in calm, modulated tones.

Frost assisted Howard to his feet and brushed him off. Howard laughed and wiped the white dust of the road from his hands.

'Quite a tumble, Master. I feel as if some lout had pulled a stool from under me.'

'I shouldn't have made you sit down.'

'I guess not.' He pulled a large multi-flanged pistol from his belt and examined it. 'Lucky the safety catch was set on my blaster or we might have been picking ourselves out of the stratosphere. Shall we be on our way?'

Frost looked his companion over; helmet, short military kilt, short sword and accoutrements slapping at his thighs. He blinked and answered. 'Yes. Yes, of course.'

As they swung into the city gates, Frost inquired, 'Do you know where you are headed?'

'Yes, certainly. To Star-Light's villa in the Grove.'

'And you know what to expect there?'

115

'Oh, you mean our discussion. I know the customs here, Master, and am quite undismayed, I assure you. Star-Light and I understand each other. She's one of these "Out of sight, out of mind" girls. Now that I'm back from Ultima Thule, she'll give up the priesthood and we'll settle down and raise a lot of fat babies.'

'Ultima Thule? Do you remember my study?'

'Of course I do – and Robert and Helen and all the rest.'

'Is that what you meant by Ultima Thule?'

'Not exactly. I can't explain it, Master. I'm a practical military man. I'll leave such things to you priests and teachers.'

They paused in front of Estelle's house. 'Coming in, Master?'

'No, I think not. I must be getting back.'

'You know best.' Howard clapped him on the shoulder. 'You have been a true friend, Master. Our first brat shall be named for you.'

'Thank you, Howard. Goodbye, and good luck to both of you.'

'And to you.' He entered the house with a confident stride.

Frost walked slowly back towards the gates, his mind preoccupied with myriad thoughts. There seemed to be no end to the permutations and combinations; either of matter, or of mind. Martha, Robert, Helen – now Howard and Estelle. It should be possible to derive a theory that would cover them all.

As he mused, his heel caught on a loose paving block and he stumbled across his easy chair.

The absence of the five students was going to be hard to explain, Frost knew – so he said nothing to anyone. The weekend passed before anyone took the absences seriously. On Monday a policeman came to his house, asking questions.

116

His answers were not illuminating, for he had reasonably refrained from trying to tell the true story. The District Attorney smelled a serious crime, kidnappings or perhaps a mass murder. Or maybe one of these love cults – you can never tell about these professors!

He caused a warrant to be issued Tuesday morning; Sergeant Izowski was sent to pick him up.

The Professor came quietly and entered the black wagon without protest. 'Look, Doc,' said the sergeant, encouraged by his docile manner, 'why don't you tell us where you hid 'em? You know we'_ bound to dig them up in time.'

Frost turned, looked him in the eyes, and smiled. 'Time,' he said softly, 'ah, time . . . yes, you could dig them up, in Time.' He then got into the wagon and sat down quietly, closed his eyes, and placed his mind in the necessary calm receptive condition.

The sergeant placed one foot on the tailboard, braced his bulk in the only door, and drew out his notebook. When he finished writing he looked up.

Professor Frost was gone.

Frost had intended to look up Howard and Estelle. Inadvertently he let his mind dwell on Helen and Robert at the crucial moment. When he 'landed' it was not in the world of the future he had visited twice before. He did not know where he was – on earth apparently, somewhere and some *when*.

It was wooded rolling country, like the hills of southern Missouri, or New Jersey. Frost had not sufficient knowledge of botany to be able to tell whether the species of trees he saw around him were familiar or not. But he was given no time to study the matter.

He heard a shout, an answering shout. Human figures came bursting out of the trees in a ragged line. He thought that they were attacking him, looked wildly around for shelter, and found none. But they kept on past him, ignoring him, except that the one who passed closest to him

117

glanced at him hastily, and shouted something. Then he, too, was gone.

Frost was left standing, bewildered, in the small natural clearing in which he had landed.

Before he had had time to integrate these events one of the fleeing figures reappeared and yelled to him, accompanying the words with a gesture unmistakable – he was to come along.

Frost hesitated. The figure ran towards and hit him with a clean tackle. The next few seconds were very confused, but he pulled himself together sufficiently to realise that he was seeing the world upside down; the stranger was carrying him at a strong dogtrot, thrown over one shoulder.

Bushes whipped at his face, then the way led downward for several yards, and he was dumped casually to the ground. He sat up and rubbed himself.

He found himself in a tunnel which ran upwards to daylight and downward the Lord knew where. Figures milled around him but ignored him. Two of them were setting up some apparatus between the group and the mouth of the tunnel. They worked with extreme urgency, completing what they were doing in seconds, and stepped back. Frost heard a soft gentle hum.

The mouth of the tunnel became slightly cloudy. He soon saw why – the apparatus was spinning a web from wall to wall, blocking the exit. The web became less tenuous, translucent, opaque. The hum persisted for minutes thereafter and the strange machine continued to weave and thicken the web. One of the figures glanced at its belt, spoke one word in the tone of command, and the humming ceased.

Frost could feel relief spread over the group like a warm glow. He felt it himself and relaxed, knowing intuitively that some acute danger had been averted.

The member of the group who had given the order to shut off the machine turned around, happened to see Frost, and approached him, asking some questions in a sweet but peremptory soprano. Frost was suddenly aware of three things; the leader was a woman, it was the leader who had rescued him, and the costume and general appearance of these people *matched that of the transformed Robert Monroe.*

A smile spread over his face. Everything was going to be all right!

The question was repeated with marked impatience. Frost felt that an answer was required, though he did not understand the language and was sure that she could not possibly know English. Nevertheless –

'Madame,' he said in English, getting to his feet and giving her a courtly bow, 'I do not know your language and do not understand your question, but I suspect that you have saved my life. I am grateful.'

She seemed puzzled and somewhat annoyed, and demanded something else – at least Frost thought it was a different question; he could not be sure. This was getting nowhere. The language difficulty was almost insuperable, he realised. It might take days, weeks, months to overcome it. In the meantime these people were busy with a war, and would be in no frame of mind to bother with a useless incoherent stranger.

He did not want to be turned out on the surface.

How annoying, he thought, how stupidly annoying! Probably Monroe and Helen were somewhere around, but he could die of old age and never find them. They might be anywhere on the planet. How would an American, dumped down in Tibet, make himself understood if his only possible interpreter were in South America? Or whereabouts unknown? How would he make the Tibetans understand that there even was an interpreter? Botheration!

Still, he must make a try. What was it Monroe had said his name was *here*? Egan – no Igor. That was it – Igor.

'Igor,' he said.

The leader cocked her head, 'Igor?' she said.

119

She turned and called out, 'Igor!' giving it the marked guttural, the liquid 'r' that Monroe had given it. A man came forward. The Professor looked eagerly at him, but he was a stranger, like the rest. The leader pointed to the man and stated, 'Igor.'

This is growing complicated, thought Frost, apparently Igor is a common name here – too common. Then he had a sudden idea:

If Monroe and Helen got through, their badly-needed chattels might have made them prominent. 'Igor,' he said, 'Helen Fisher.'

The leader was attentive at once, her face alive. ' "Elen Feesher?" ' she repeated.

'Yes, yes – Helen Fisher.'

She stood quiet, thinking. It was plain that the words meant something to her. She clapped her hands together and spoke, commandingly. Two men stepped forward. She addressed them rapidly for several moments.

The two men stepped up to Frost, each taking an arm. They started to lead him away. Frost held back for a moment and said over his shoulder, 'Helen Fisher?'

'Elen Fesher! ' the leader assured him. He had to be content with that.

Two hours passed, more or less. He had not been mistreated and the room in which they had placed him was comfortable but it was a cell – at least the door was fastened. Perhaps he had said the wrong thing, perhaps those syllables meant something quite different here from a simple proper name.

The room in which he found himself was bare and lighted only by a dim glow from the walls, as had all of this underground world which he had seen so far. He was growing tired of the place and was wondering whether or not it would do any good to set up a commotion when he heard someone at the door.

The door slid back; he saw the leader, a smile on her rather grim, middle-aged features. She spoke in her own tongue, then added, 'Igor . . . Ellenfeesher.'

He followed her.

Glowing passageways, busy squares where he was subjected to curious stares, an elevator which startled him by dropping suddenly when he was not aware that it *was* an elevator, and finally a capsule-like vehicle in which they were sealed airtight and which went somewhere very fast indeed to judge by the sudden surge of weight when it started and again when it stopped – through them all he followed his guide, not understanding and lacking means of inquiring. He tried to relax and enjoy the passing moment, as his companion seemed to bear him no ill-will, though her manner was brusque – that of a person accustomed to giving orders and not in the habit of encouraging casual intimacy.

They arrived at a door which she opened and strode in. Frost followed and was almost knocked off his feet by a figure which charged into him and grasped him with both arms. 'Doctor! Doctor Frost! '

It was Helen Fisher, dressed in the costume worn by both sexes here. Behind her stood Robert – or Igor, his gnome-like face widened with a grin.

He detached Helen's arm gently. 'My dear,' he said inanely, 'imagine finding you here.'

'Imagine finding you here,' she retorted. 'Why Professor – you're crying!'

'Oh, no, not at all,' he said hastily, and turned to Monroe. 'It's good to see you, too, Robert.'

'That goes double for me. Doc,' Monroe agreed.

The leader said something to Monroe. He answered her rapidly in their tongue and turned to Frost. 'Doctor, this is my elder sister, Margri, Actoon Margri – Major Margri, you might translate it roughly.'

'She has been very kind to me,' said Frost, and bowed to her, acknowledging the introduction. Margri clapped her hands smartly together at the waist and ducked her head, features impassive.

'She gave the salute of equals,' explained Robert-Igor.

'I translated the title doctor as best I could which causes her to assume that your rank is the same as hers.'

'What should I do?'

'Return it.'

Frost did so, awkwardly.

Doctor Frost brought his erstwhile students up to 'date' – using a term which does not apply, since they were on a different time axis. His predicament with the civil authorities brought a cry of dismay from Helen. 'Why, you poor thing! How awful of them! '

'Oh, I wouldn't say so,' protested Frost. 'It was reasonable so far as they knew. But I'm afraid I can't go back.'

'You don't need to,' Igor assured him. 'You're more than welcome here.'

'Perhaps I can help out in your war.'

'Perhaps – but you've already done more than anyone here by what you've enabled me to do. We are working on it now.' He swung his arm in a gesture which took in the whole room.

Igor had been detached from combat duty and assigned to staff work, in order to make available earth techniques. Helen was helping. 'Nobody believes my story but my sister,' he admitted, 'but I've been able to show them enough for them to realise that what I've got is important, so they've given me a free hand and are practically hanging over my shoulder, waiting to see what we can produce. I've already got them started on a jet fighter and attack rockets to arm it.'

Frost expressed surprise. How could so much be done so fast? Were the time rates different? Had Helen and Igor crossed over many weeks before, figured along this axis?

No, he was told, but Igor's countrymen, though lacking many earth techniques, were far ahead of earth in manufacturing skill. They used a single general type of machine to manufacture almost anything. They fed into it a plan which Igor call for want of a better term the

122

blueprints – it was in fact, a careful scale model of the device to be manufactured; the machine retooled itself and produced the artifact. One of them was, at that moment, moulding the bodies of fighting planes out of plastic, all in one piece and in one operation.

'We are going to arm these jobs with both the stasis ray and rockets,' said Igor. 'Freeze 'em and then shoot the damn things down while they are out of control.'

They talked a few minutes, but Frost could see that Igor was getting fidgety. He guessed the reason, and asked to be excused. Igor seized on the suggestion. 'W? will see you a little later,' he said with relief. 'I'll have some one dig up quarters for you. We *are* pretty rushed. War work – I know you'll understand.'

Frost fell asleep that night planning how he could help his two young friends, and their friends, in their struggle.

But it did not work out that way. His education had been academic rather than practical; he discovered that the reference books which Igor and Helen had brought along were so much Greek to him – worse, for he understood Greek. He was accorded all honour and a comfortable living because of Igor's affirmation that he had been the invaluable agent whereby this planet had received the invaluable new weapons, but he soon realised that for the job at hand he was useless, not even fit to act as an interpreter.

He was a harmless nuisance, a pensioner – and he knew it.

And underground life got on his nerves. The ever-present light bothered him. He had an unreasoned fear of radioactivity, born of ignorance, and Igor's reassurances did not stifle the fear. The war depressed him. He was not temperamentally cut out to stand up under the nervous tension of war. His helplessness to aid in the war effort, his lack of companionship, and his idleness all worked to increase his malaise.

He wandered into Igor and Helen's workroom one day,

hoping for a moment's chat, if they were not too busy. They were not. Igor was pacing up and down, Helen followed them with worried eyes.

He cleared his throat. 'Uh – I say, something the matter?

Igor nodded, answered, 'Quite a lot,' and dropped back into his preoccupation.

'It's like this,' said Helen, 'in spite of the new weapons, things are still going against us. Igor is trying to figure out what to try next.'

'Oh, I see. Sorry.' He started to leave.

'Don't go. Sit down.' He did so, and started mulling the matter over in his mind. It was annoying, very annoying!

'I'm afraid I'm not much use to you,' he said at last to Helen. 'Too bad Howard Jenkins isn't here.'

'I don't suppose it matters,' she answered. 'We have the cream of modern earth engineering in these books.'

'I don't mean that. I mean Howard himself, as he is where he's gone. They had a little gadget there in the future called a blaster. I gathered that it was a very powerful weapon indeed.'

Igor caught some of this and whirled around. 'What was it? How did it work?'

'Why, really,' said Frost, 'I can't say. I'm not up on such things, you know. I gathered that it was sort of a disintegrating ray.'

'Can you sketch it? Think, man, think! '

Frost tried. Presently he stopped an. said, 'I'm afraid this isn't any good. I don't remember clearly and anyhow I don't know anything about the inside of it.'

Igor sighed, sat down, and ran his hand through his hair.

After some minutes of gloomy silence, Helen said, 'Couldn't we go get it?'

'Eh? How's that? How would you find him?'

'Could you find him, Professor?'

Frost sat up. 'I don't know,' he said slowly, '– but I'll try! '

There was the city. Yes, and there was the same gate he .lad passed through once before. He hurried on.

Star-Light was glad to see him, but not particularly surprised. Frost wondered if anything could surprise this dreamy girl. But Howard more than made up for her lack of enthusiasm. He pounded Frost's back hard enough to cause pleurisy. 'Welcome home, Master! Welcome home! I didn't know whether or not you would ever come, but we are ready for you. I had a room built for you and you alone, in case you ever showed up. What do you think of that? You are to live with us, you know. No sense in ever going back to that grubby school.'

Frost thanked him, but added, 'I came on business. I need your help, urgently.'

'You do? Well, tell me, man, tell me! '

Frost explained. 'So you see, I've got to take the secret of your blaster back to them. They need it. They must have it.'

'And they shall have it,' agreed Howard.
Some time later the problem looked more complicated. Try as he would Frost was simply not able to soak up the technical knowledge necessary to be able to take the secret back. The pedagogical problem presented was as great as if an untutored savage were to be asked to comprehend radio engineering sufficiently to explain to engineers unfamiliar with radio how to build a major station. And Frost was by no means sure that he could take a blaster with him through the country of Time.

'Well,' said Howard at last, 'I shall simply have to go with you.'

Star-Light, who had listened quietly, showed her first acute interest. 'Darling! You must not –'

'Stop it,' said Howard, his chin set stubbornly. 'This is a matter of obligation and duty. You keep out of it.'

125

Frost felt the acute embarrassment one always feels when forced to overhear a husband and wife having a difference of opinion.

When they were ready, Frost took Howard by the wrist. 'Look me in the eyes,' he said. 'You remember how we did it before?'

Howard was trembling. 'I remember. Master, do you think you can do it – and not lose me?'

'I hope so,' said Frost, 'now relax.'

They got back to the chamber from which Frost had started, a circumstance which Frost greeted with relief. It would have been awkward to have to cross half a planet to find his friends. He was not sure yet just how the spatial dimensions fitted into the time dimensions. Some day he would have to study the matter, work out an hypothesis and try to check it.

Igor and Howard wasted little time on social amenities. They were deep into engineering matters before Helen had finished greeting the Professor.

At long last – 'There,' said Howard, 'I guess that covers everything. I'll leave my blaster for a model. Any more questions?'

'No,' said Igor, 'I understand it, and I've got every word you've said recorded. I wonder if you know what this means to us, old man? It unquestionably will win the war for us.'

'I can guess,' said Howard. 'This little gadget is the mainstay of our systemwide pax. Ready, Doctor. I'm getting kinda anxious.'

But you're not going, Doctor?' cried Helen. It was both a question and a protest.

'I've got to guide him back,' said Frost.

'Yes,' Howard confirmed, 'but he is staying to live with us. Aren't you, Master?'

'Oh, no! ' It was Helen again.

Igor put an arm around her. 'Don't coax him,' he told her. 'You know he has not been happy here. I gather

126

that Howard's home would suit him better. If so, he's earned it.'

Helen thought about it, then came up to Frost, placed both hands on his shoulders, and kissed him, standing on tiptoe to do so. 'Goodbye, Doc,' she said in a choky voice, 'or anyhow, *au revoir!* '

He reached up and patted one of her hands.

Frost lay in the sun, letting the rays soak into his old bones. It was certainly pleasant here. He missed Helen and Igor a little, but he suspected that they did not really miss him. And life with Howard and Star-Light was more to his liking. Officially he was tutor to their children, if and when. Actually he was just as lazy and useless as he had always wanted to be, with time on his hands. Time . . . Time.

There was just one thing that he would liked to have known: What did Sergeant Izowski say when he looked up and saw that the police wagon was empty? Probably thought it was impossible.

It did not matter. He was too lazy and sleepy to care. Time enough for a little nap before lunch. Time enough . . .

Time.

SCIENCE FICTION

MONTHLY*

A COLOURFUL NEW MAGAZINE-REVIEW

**Short stories, features, interviews and reviews
covering the whole sphere of science-fiction.**

First issue on sale January 31 , Price 25p

Available at newsagents and bookstalls everywhere, or, if you should have any
difficulty in obtaining your copy, available from the publishers,
New English Library Ltd., price 30p (inclusive of postage and packing.)

TO YOUR LOCAL NEWSAGENT

**Please take note of my order for a regular monthly copy of
'SCIENCE-FICTION MONTHLY'.**

Name ....

Address ....

....

Price 25p monthly — First tremendous issue on sale January 31

NEW ENGLISH LIBRARY LIMITED
Barnard's Inn, Holborn, London EC1N 2JR. Tel: 01–405 4614.
